THE SOUTH RECLAIMED

RACHEL DRUMMOND

ODYSSEY
BOOKS

Published by Odyssey Books in 2016

ISBN 978-1-922200-56-3

www.odysseybooks.com.au

A Cataloguing-in-Publication entry is available from the National Library of Australia

ISBN: 978-1-922200-56-3 (pbk)

ISBN: 978-1-922200-57-0 (ebook)

This book is dedicated to the memory of Torres vs. Zombies.
The first of our podcast family to be lost to the hordes.

A moment of silence for our fallen and those who will follow.

Prologue

It was the thick walls that had saved them. Walls that had kept prisoners contained since the city had been founded now kept death at arm's length. Before the plane had come, before fire had rained down on the corpses that roamed the street, the small group had fled to the bluestone walls that only held the memory of death. The cells became home, and for once the occupants were not desperate to escape them.

Meghan had been the one to suggest the gaol, dragging her partner, Josh, and his friends from their house when she had seen their neighbours eaten. She had tried to call her father to warn them, but they had refused to come, insisting that what was happening was not real, it was just another skirmish. That it would all be over soon because the police would intervene and stem the riots. She had not waited for them, instinct telling her that there was no winning this battle. Josh had been sceptical at first too—it had taken seeing his brother torn into pieces to convince him otherwise. Meghan had nearly lost him then when he had tried to wrest his arm from her hand to save him. His shock, and her panic, had been enough to pull him away from the teenager's grasping hand.

Matt had been the one to suggest a foray into the hospital across the road. The need for food and medical equipment was growing as the days passed with no sign of the end. They had watched the parade of the dead, waiting for the right time. This had put them in prime position to watch as another group snuck out the door, breaking into a car to smash through the barracks fence beside them.

Meghan had wanted to call to them—the first new faces they had seen since they had sought refuge. Josh had stopped her, pointing out that there was no way of knowing if these people could be trusted. Not wanting to go against the group, who were all in agreement with not hailing the new group, Meghan had shut her mouth. They had watched in silence as the new group had commandeered what looked like a tank and left the city in their wake.

Her father had been right in the end. The government had intervened. They had responded with explosions.

Josh had suggested finding a way to the roof, to let them know that there were survivors in the building. Meghan had allowed the promise of rescue to bloom, only to watch as the fragile assurance was swallowed up in the fire. They fled to the lower levels, praying for the walls to hold. The concussion rolled through the gaol, shaking them roughly and forcing them to hold on to one another for support.

The shaking didn't confine itself to shaking the people; the foundations of the gaol were tested to their limits, cracks fissuring up the aged mortar as the bomb did what time had failed to do.

The walls crumbled.

This time, Meghan did not hold her tongue. If the rest of the group didn't want to come, she would leave in the last tank on her own.

This time, there was no argument.

Chapter One
The Aftermath

Of the dozen or so who had escaped the prison, precious few remained. They hid in the bowels of the stadium that still clawed at the smoky sky above the city; their world had been reduced to a number they could count with their shoes still on. The air still held on to the smoke that had blanketed the city a little over a month before.

Sarah stepped out of the blessedly cold bathroom. Showering had become a luxury they could no longer indulge in, so she took every opportunity she could to sponge off the grime that clung to her skin. Self-imposed water restrictions allowed them little more than a wet rag to combat it, but she took what she could.

She hummed mindlessly, taking comfort in the gentle tune of her mother's favourite hymn as she dried herself off. It bounced off the cold walls, echoing through the air.

Sarah had lived a single life for so long, filling every spare minute with work, studies and the monotony of day-to-day life, that she had never truly realised what it meant to be alone until now.

Echoed footsteps broke through her singing and she trailed off into silence, turning to face the narrow steps that led down to the washroom.

'Don't stop on my account. At least you can carry a tune,'

Meghan joked as she stepped inside, her brown hair tossed up in a clip on the top of her head. Since saving Sarah from under the car, the women had grown close, their friendship increasing as their group dwindled down to five at the hands of the infected, and the sweeping fires that had destabilised most of the buildings in which they had tried to find shelter.

'Hmm?' Sarah looked up, embarrassed at the attention. 'Just the magic of good acoustics, that's all.'

Meghan unwrapped the ragged towel from her slender form and stepped up to the bucket, eyeing the water suspiciously. 'The boys haven't beaten us to it today?'

Sarah shook her head.

'I made sure I put my hand up for wash house duty today—we got to it first.' She winked at the taller girl, holding up the cracked bar of soap and a tattered piece of towel.

Meghan took it eagerly, dunking it in the still clear cool water and resting the wet rag on her face with a sigh. 'I miss scented body wash,' she whined softly, the cloth muffling her voice.

The cool room was the only place that gave them respite from the summer heat. Despite recent heavy rains, the sun still heated up everything around them to uncomfortable levels.

Sarah stood up to leave.

'Hang around a bit. It's nice to have the company of another woman in this pool of testosterone. It's a wonder we don't start growing beards just from proximity.' She swiped the cool cloth down her neck and looked over at Sarah.

'It's bad enough we smell like the guys, don't wish that on us as well!' Sarah laughed. She moved to the small bench that ran along the wall, leaning back against the cool bricks and shutting her eyes. 'Do you think Darwin was right?' she mused.

'What do you mean?' Meghan handed the cloth to Sarah and turned away.

Sarah distractedly cleaned Meghan's back. 'Survival of the fittest. Do you think the people who will make it through this are the strong ones? The brave ones?' She paused, suddenly struck by a horrifying thought. 'Are we going to have a predominantly male population when all this is done?'

Meghan smiled, looking over her shoulder. 'Not a woman's lib supporter then?' she asked.

'I see myself as more of a realist,' Sarah said, frowning.

Meghan stood again, moving back to the bucket of water, submerging the cloth and cleaning off her legs in languid strokes.

'Some women have no idea how to survive without their nail salons or shopping trips—most have no idea how to live in the bush.' she scoffed. 'Can you imagine them having to skin and gut an animal just to eat?'

Meghan laughed at the mental image. 'Don't you think you might be being a little hard on your own sex? I've seen men just as hung up on the comforts of modern day life.' She swung her towel over her shoulders and sat beside Sarah on the bench.

Sarah rested her head on the wall behind her, looking up at the high ceiling. 'I think equality is all well and good, but there are things that men and women are naturally geared towards. That's not to say they *can't* do those things,' she insisted, looking over at her brunette friend, worried that she may have caused offence.

Meghan waved her on.

'Traditionally, men are *supposed* to be stronger than women,' she explained weakly. Sarah thought back to what she had been through with James, the ease with which he picked up a tool she had struggled with.

'I get what you mean,' Meghan said, letting Sarah drop the poorly attempted explanation. 'So what makes *us* survivors, do you think?'

Sarah shrugged. 'I think the ones who survive will be the ones who know how to use their brains *and* their boobs.'

The dying sea of grass was mostly bathed in sunlight. A low haze of smoke stuck in their throats as the two women walked towards a patch ensconced in the shadow of the stadium walls where Josh was crouched over a small fire, watching a small pot carefully.

'Good to see they can manage that much,' Meghan whispered to Sarah, who snorted indelicately. 'Where are the others?' she asked Josh.

He glanced up at them before looking back at the small portion of rice in the pot. 'They went to see if there was anything else we could scavenge from out there.' He swept a hand vaguely behind him, towards the high walls that surrounded them.

Along the city side of the grounds, in stark contrast to the haze that still hung heavily above them, the white spires of the sports ground rose like exposed ribs. Much of the smoke was from the smaller fires that still ran unchecked through the city's abandoned buildings, the aftermath of the bomb that had landed on the city outskirts. Narrowly escaping the initial blast, the group had huddled within the high walls of the prison, praying they would hold.

Sarah had almost wept in thanks when the first clap of thunder rolled through the air, and they had all climbed to the highest point along the walls to watch as the heavy rain broke through the heat to drench the worst of the fires.

From their position, they could see the still-smoking crater just past the city. Sarah pictured the sprawling grounds that she had witnessed most of her working life, now reduced to rubble in her mind's eye.

The infected had not been excluded from the devastation. Charred figures with blackened skin paraded past them constantly. Most were reduced to crawling after the rampant fires had eaten their legs down to a scorched mess, unable to hold them upright. Many had severed limbs, or bones clearly pulverised beneath the skin from the shockwave. Sarah had seen one with no face, its sparse hair a black wiry mess atop a bloody skull—what remained of the face looked like a melted candle. The air had been thick with the stench of burnt flesh for days.

Sarah had felt sick. Not, as she would have thought, because of the cloying smell, but because her empty stomach and traitorous brain had taken the opportunity to remind her of her mother's roast pork dinners.

They were all starving; the meagre food supplies they had been able to bring with them had barely lasted four days, and the water all but gone before the rains had come. They had caught what they could in buckets found in the clubrooms, and had hurriedly pegged tarps over the grounds and weighted them in the middle, watching gleefully as the rain filled each one.

Matt and Jim had gone out, foraging the closer shops when the food had started to run out. They came back almost empty handed. The shops that would have held food had already been picked clean, or destroyed by the explosion and the ensuing fires. They had been lucky to find a small bag of white rice and a few small cans of unwanted food, which Jim had taken great pride in displaying on the table before whipping out a half-melted chocolate bar from his pocket. It had been broken up and distributed with the type of panache usually reserved for a rare steak.

Sarah closed her eyes and sighed in bliss as the memory of the dark chocolate melting on her tongue replayed in her head; she had taken tiny bites to prolong the experience. It had not lasted anywhere near long enough. None of the food had. The bag of rice was half-empty now, even with the strict rations they had been allocating.

'What do you think their chances are?' Sarah asked, pulling her mind back to the present.

Josh shrugged. 'Honestly? I think we've more than outstayed our welcome here.' He took the small pot from the fire, spooning out five small portions onto chipped plates. 'Everything has been completely emptied. We may have to think about moving on soon.'

'Where to?' Meghan picked at the small plate slowly, savouring each mouthful. Josh was less delicate, eating his own tiny portion far too quickly, and looking disappointed when it was gone. 'Is there any safe place left?'

Sarah looked up from her plate. 'What about the Grampians?' she asked.

Josh looked at her quizzically. 'What about them?'

'When we had the radios set up at home, we were in touch with a few other groups of survivors. I think one said they were headed up there. There was a refugee camp being set up.'

'I think Matt's been camping around there,' Josh mused. 'We'll ask him what he thinks when they get back.'

'Ooh, food!' Matt's cheerful voice broke through the conversation, followed by a hand that snatched up one of the remaining plates. Jim picked up the last and they tucked in quickly.

'Slim pickings?' Josh asked rhetorically.

Matt tried to speak through his mouthful of rice but a glance at Meghan's scowl convinced him to swallow first. 'Nothing. The shops are impossible to get to now. The buildings are gutted.'

Josh picked up the near empty bag of rice, weighing it sceptically. 'This isn't going to last much longer, a day or two at the most.'

'So we move on then.' Matt pushed his empty plate to the side.

Josh nodded. 'Preferably soon. Matt, how well do you know the Grampians?'

Matt waggled his hand. 'I've been climbing there once, did a bit of hunting.'

'Hunting?' Sarah asked curiously.

'There's heaps of deer out there.'

Josh's eyes glazed over, no doubt salivating at the thought of fresh meat.

'Sarah said there might be a refugee camp up there.' Meghan stood and started to collect the plates.

'*May* be,' Sarah emphasised. 'We couldn't get in contact with the other group after they left.'

'Fine, *may* be. It's still more then we have now.' Josh brushed off, handing his plate to Meghan. She stacked them beside the small bucket they had been using for the dishes, the water greying a little with overuse.

Meghan wrinkled her nose disdainfully. 'Should I swap the water out?' she asked, not really wanting to use up their drinking water unnecessarily.

'No, leave it. The dishes too. If we're going, it needs to be as soon as we can.' Josh stood up and stretched. 'Let's use what's left of the light to pack up the truck and figure out how to get out of the city.'

Matt shot a look at Jim. 'We know the roads.'

'No. We know our destination,' Jim corrected. 'Did you see the roads at all when we were out there?' he shot back. 'We can't make a plan when we don't know which roads are still useable. A map with several options, or at least a general idea wouldn't hurt.' He looked at them expectantly.

'Now?' Meghan asked, surprised.

'Waiting's not working in our favour,' he pointed out.

It didn't take long to pack their depleted supplies into the Bushmaster they had taken from the reservist base before heading to the gaol. Meghan had watched the strangers escape from the dark hospital, level the fence and escape in one of the heavy trucks that would have transported them all. The walls had kept them safe so far, holding the hordes at bay. The heavy plane that had dropped the explosives, blowing up half the city and almost taken down gaol walls, had quickly changed their minds. They'd followed suit within the hour and relocated to the stadium.

What sleep they got that night was unsettled and sporadic. When morning came, it was a bleary-eyed Josh who slipped into the driver's seat. Meghan took her place next to him while Sarah, Matt and Jim found seats in the back.

Josh slowly guided the heavy truck through the choked roads, moving as slowly as he could to avoid the dead vehicles littering the way. Every now and then, a thump echoed through the tinny structure as the blackened corpses drew close enough to pound at the sides.

They had not made it too far down the road before they reached a dead end, cut off entirely by the piled up debris of crumpled cars and abandoned belongings, the bridge beyond it out of their reach. Josh pressed down on the brakes, slowing the Bushmaster to a halt.

Jim pushed his head between the seats, pointing out a smaller road to their right, across the median strip. 'Turn down there.'

'That's a one-way road,' Josh pointed out.

Jim shot him a disbelieving look. 'Right, so be careful to avoid the many oncoming cars that are sure to *not* be there.'

Josh scowled back, pushing the accelerator again to bump the truck over the curb. 'Some of us actually have decent driving habits that are a little tough to break,' he muttered.

The Bushmaster pushed across the highway, mowing down several grotesque figures in front of them, their rotting flesh no match for the sturdy truck. Josh turned down the small road, squashed between a car yard and the tall windows of a car tinting shop, the truck's width blocking off the road entirely. As they neared the end of the road where it terminated at the freeway, Josh slowed the truck again, speaking over his shoulder to Jim.

'The road's completely blocked, we'll never get through that!'

Jim climbed onto the seat and pushed open the hatch in the roof. He stuck his head outside briefly, then slipped back down. 'There's a road up on your left. Take that and follow it around.'

The 'road' proved to be little wider than a residential driveway, and the driving skills needed to manoeuvre it would not have been out of place on a rally driver's circuit. More than once, the inhabitants of the truck winced as the metal scraped loudly on the bricks as it squeezed past.

'I'm so glad I've never driven with you before this,' Meghan muttered, her knuckles white from tightly gripping her seat.

'I've never driven like this before!' he defended quickly.

'Well, we appreciate your newly developed delinquent tendencies now.' Jim rested a hand on his seat and nodded sombrely.

The small road took them under the bridge and around to the

city-bound lanes. Swinging out onto the freeway, he nosed his way between the motionless cars.

The lane had remained relatively clear, the too-high concrete median strip stopping the outward-bound cars from moving back across in their doomed bid to escape across the river and out of the city.

Jim reached between the front seats as Josh drove, flicking on the radio and filling the truck with the hiss of static.

'What are you doing?' Meghan asked.

'Sarah said she found the group that went to the Grampians on the radio. Maybe we can find them again, or someone else who may have made it.' He kept shifting through channels as he spoke, the pitch whining slightly with each change.

'... 'nother tourist, not sure how far out.'

They jumped at the garbled male voice.

'Ahh-ha-ha!' Jim exclaimed, grabbing for the handset.

Sarah stood up behind him and grabbed the back of his shirt, yanking him away from the radio. 'Wait! Make sure it's a friendly group first. Please?' She was equally surprised at the new voice, the first she had heard in weeks, but the bikers she had seen with James during their foray to the camping store, had made her wary about unfamiliar groups.

'She's right. Wait a bit,' Josh agreed.

Jim pouted, but rested his still outstretched hand on the back of Josh's seat.

A female voice came through the speakers next. *Can you make out numbers? And what type of vehicles?*

'I see a single four-wheel-drive, with … maybe three occupants.'

Meghan looked back at Sarah. 'Why would they ask about the type of car?' she asked.

Sarah shrugged. 'Maybe to see if it's worth taking?'

'Ahh, highway robbery, when crimes were simple and obvious.' Matt sighed in exaggerated whimsy beside her.

The female voice came back through the speakers. *'How far are they from here?'*

'Just passing Langi Ghiran.'

'I know that area,' Matt said. 'We've camped around there often enough. It's just outside of Ararat, near the Grampians.'

'Can you cut them off at the lake?' the woman asked, her voice adopting a sharp, slightly worried edge. *'We don't want them any closer than the city without checking them out.'*

Jim reached out once more, picking up the handset. He glanced around at the others, seeking any objections before he depressed the button on the side.

'Um … Hello?' he spoke hesitantly into the mouthpiece. The others seemed to hold their breath.

Josh tore his eyes from the road long enough to glare at him. 'Yes, very eloquent, well done,' he scoffed. Jim ignored him.

'Who the hell is this?' The female voice no longer sounded concerned, the anger was clear even over the grainy soundwaves.

Sarah flinched at the tone.

'We … that is … my friends and me, we're in Geelong. We were in contact with another group over the radio before the bomb. They said they were headed out to a refugee camp up in the Grampians …' Trailing off into uncertainty, Jim looked helplessly at Sarah. She shrugged unhelpfully.

There was silence over the radio before the male voice came through once more. *'A bomb? Seriously, a fucking bomb? What the hell happened?'*

'We're not too sure,' Jim replied slowly.

Sarah stayed silent. So far she had managed to keep what they had heard over the radio from the others, unsure how they would respond. She wasn't about to tell total strangers over the radio.

'*These people you spoke to, they may have come through here, but we had heavy losses when some bright spark brought the infection into the camp with them,*' said a new voice. '*Half of us got wiped out, and half of those who survived pissed off with most of our supplies. We've put some very heavy checks and quarantines in place since.*'

'*Blue!*' the woman interrupted sharply. '*These* strangers *don't need to know our business.*' Her sharp tone was not lost on the group.

'*I just want them to understand why you … why* we're *a little suspicious of new people,*' the unseen male defended. The silence grew uncomfortable as it stretched on.

Meghan plucked the handset from Jim's hand. 'Look, we're sorry about what happened, and we understand why you wouldn't want more newcomers thrown at you. Could you at least point us in a direction where we might find somewhere to regroup?'

The woman snorted. '*There is nowhere else. We haven't heard anything since the HMAS* Canberra *left port about a week ago. I think they were headed out to Tasmania.*'

'*Ruby.*' The man's calm voice seemed to soothe her a little as she sighed heavily.

'*If you can make it to Ararat, and let our guys check you over …*' She hesitated, clearly struggling with the thought of inviting new people in. '*… we will discuss it then.*' The warning tone was clear, even if the words went unsaid.

Meghan brought the mouthpiece up again. 'We understand. Will you be on this channel so we can let you know when we arrive?'

'Probably not. We cycle through so no one is tempted by the thought of easy targets. Keep driving, we'll know when you get close.'

'Thank you, Ruby, and ...' Meghan hesitated, having forgotten the man's name.

'Blue. Don't you mind Rube. Her sister was one of the people who cleared us out.'

'Piss off.' Ruby was agitated, clearly not wanting to relive that memory.

Blue must have been used to her dark mood because he seemed to brush her off. *'If we don't get to you before you reach the town, stay near the lake and we'll meet you there. I have to go pick up this lot now.'* He signed off quickly.

Josh pulled off to the side of the road, steering carefully to nudge at a car in front of him.

'What's up, Josh?'

'I figured we should pick up some stuff to replace what we've lost.' He pointed to the huge red and blue sign for a manchester shop in front of them.

'Are you looking to take up knitting? Are you *that* bored?' Meghan teased.

'Actually I was looking at the sign below it, for the camping shop, but now that you mention it, it's not a bad idea.' He smirked at her, posturing a little. 'It'll give you girls something to do while we do our manly stuff.'

Meghan flushed and smacked his arm.

'It's not a bad idea actually. We're going to have to repair our clothes, and it might be good to have something practical to trade.'

'Why don't we just get alcohol then?' Meghan frowned.

'How long do you think that will last with this lot?' Sarah laughed. 'Plus, I reckon everyone else is going to be thinking the same thing. It might set us up as a higher priority if we have something nobody else does.' Meghan still looked put out. 'Not to mention, I think the boys need to learn to sew too.'

'What?' Matt squeaked. 'But that's a girls ...'

Meghan spun around to face him, fixing him with a glare. 'Finish it. I dare you.'

Matt shut his mouth.

'I'll go with Jim to the manchester shop and see what I can find. Meghan, you go with Josh to get what we need from the camping shop. Keep in mind that we don't have a lot of space, and we might have to walk at some point.' It felt surreal, repeating what she had told her brother when they had made the same run before their world went to hell.

'What about me?' Matt asked.

'We need you to stay here with the truck. Warn us if we have to get out quickly.'

Jim hopped out the back of the truck, cricket bat in hand. Meghan and Josh had already climbed down, when Matt grabbed Sarah's shoulders, pulling her back to face him.

'Be careful,' he said.

Sarah bit her lip and nodded, taking Jim's hand as he helped her down. She looked back up at Matt. 'Jump on the horn if we need to get out. It'll probably be too late to hide our presence at that point and it's better to have a clear warning so we can get out quickly.' She turned to follow Jim to the dark store.

Sarah was surprised when the doors remained shut at their approach, just managing to stop before her face met the glass.

'The power lines must be down somewhere around here,' Jim muttered, wedging his fingers between the sliding doors and wriggling them slightly to crack the doors open. Sarah slipped through and squinted into the dark as her eyes adjusted to the unlit interior. Jim pushed her aside softly as he made his way through to join her, shutting the doors behind them.

The dark room looked alien in the dim light. Sarah could feel the first curl of fear tug at her spine.

'Do we really need this?' she said, second-guessing her idea.

'It was a good call,' Jim reassured her. 'There are things here that we'll need. Even if clothes really aren't going to be anyone's priority.' He smirked at Sarah. 'It's better to see what we could use now, before someone else gets their hands on it. Plus, the camping shop is more likely to be looted than the haberdashery counter. If the others aren't able to find tents, this is our best chance at rigging up something on our own.'

'Then let's make this quick.' She moved to the aisle on their left, Jim shadowing her closely. As they reached the end of the row Sarah froze, straining her ears. She was sure she could hear a harsh shuffling noise that seemed to be coming from just out of sight.

Jim moved in front of her and peered around the corner, bringing the cricket bat up to his shoulder. Something was definitely behind the shelves, but he couldn't see what it was. Moving slowly, he stepped out from behind the shelves, holding his breath as a low, bestial growl rattled through the air around him.

'Was that a growl? Do those things growl?' he asked, his voice sounding painfully loud in his ears after the sustained silence.

Sarah jumped as she heard the growl again, closer this time. Shocked, she stepped backwards into the shelves. A stack of propped curtain rods teetered backwards. She reached out a desperate hand to steady them just a fraction too late. She watched in horror as the stack tipped past their balance point and clattered loudly to the ground.

The pair froze, eyes fixed on the now scattered poles at their feet. The growling stopped suddenly, a shadow detaching itself from the wall and scurrying frantically across the floor in front of them. Sarah couldn't stop the shriek that escaped her lungs. She stepped back onto the poles, skidding slightly as they rolled underfoot. Jim grabbed her arm and yanked her back up, staring incredulously in the direction of the shadow.

'Huh, I didn't know that possums growled.' His voice was strained and breathy from surprise. Sarah gave a hysterical giggle as she tried to regain her own breath. The skittering noise came again from the direction the possum had vanished but they ignored it, unwilling to waste any more time.

With their attention fixed once more on the supplies they had come for, the clawed hand that groped at her leg caught Sarah by surprise. She looked down into the milky eyes of a ghastly figure. Its throat had been torn almost completely out, with what remained of the white ridges of its trachea exposed in the gaping wound. Sarah danced back a step, panicked heat prickling across her brow and down her spine. The figure's lower half was still hidden in the shadow of the shelves.

Sarah crouched, grabbing a curtain rod at her feet. Jabbing down quickly, she speared it through the dead woman's eye with a wet squelch, stilling it instantly. Pulling her pant leg from now motionless fingers, she walked to the walls of fabric. Although her eyes had grown used to the dark, everything was limited to various shades of grey. Fingers plucked at the rolls of cotton, piling them in a heap on a piece of fabric she pulled from a nearby roll. Tying it swag style, she thrust the bundle into Jim's hands.

'Wait here,' she whispered, darting into the maze of shelves deeper into the store.

'Sarah, no! *Wait!*' he hissed after her, arms heavy with the pilfered material. 'Sarah?'

She wasn't gone long, grabbing what she thought they might need before running back within three minutes. She could see Jim's shadow, the line of his back and neck rigid as he stood in the oppressive darkness. His fingers twitched, clearly wanting to drop the bundle and head after her to drag her back to the truck.

'Let's go.' Sarah stepped out from the shadows, startling a gasp out of him.

'What the hell?' he whispered angrily. 'You dump this on me and disappear? How was I supposed to defend myself if there was more of them?'

'I'm sorry. But the cotton's going to be bloody useless without these.' She held up a shopping basket half filled with sewing paraphernalia.

He scowled at her. 'We're finding trade items, not starting a sewing club,' he bit out, still sounding sore at her perceived abandonment.

'That's exactly what these are!'

A shrill alarm cut through the air, followed by a frantic beeping noise. They both looked towards the doors.

'What the …' Sarah started, breaking off as recognition hit them both.

'The truck!'

'Matt!'

The skittering possum scratched across the floor in the darkness once more, with dragging moans in its wake. Clutching desperately at their spoils, the pair ran for the doors.

Chapter Two

Outside Ballarat

Breathe in
   Sight the target
      Breathe out slowly
         Pull back, rest finger under chin

The slender shaft quivered in steady fingers.

Release

The arrow flew through the air, seeking out its target before burying its point in the heavyset woman's chest with a heavy *thunk*. She snarled at them through a shattered jaw as they drew closer to examine the shot.

'Good! You're getting better!' Joe plucked the compound bow from Luke's fingers and walked over to pull the arrow from the bloody torso before guiding Luke back to the group. Joe had been teaching Luke the finer points of archery to take his mind off the destroyed city behind them.

They had been sent off from Meredith by a massive storm that had swept up out of nowhere, drenching the fields around them and softening the hard-packed earth underfoot. The orange glow that had reflected off the sky over Geelong had thankfully dimmed a little under the belting rain.

Their slow progress to the outskirts of the Gold Rush town of Ballarat had been, for the most part, uneventful. Although the roads were relatively clear of cars, sheep and cattle from the neighbouring farmlands had wandered across many of the roads, and felled trees and limbs blocked their path. The huge Bushmaster had made easy work of the bordering paddocks in the places where the road had been completely cut off, but the campervan was made of less sturdy stuff and needed to be hauled by the military vehicle through some of the muddier areas.

The remains of a large grey kangaroo still smoked over the low fire. Esther had already curled up in the front seat of the Bushmaster, preferring to sleep where she was guaranteed solid protection. Both of the larger vehicles had been angled to provide a wall to two sides of the camp; one of the tarps was strung out to provide shelter while they nestled in between. The third side was blocked by a second tarp hung mainly to keep the light inside. They had discussed moving the four-wheel-drive in front, but in the end had decided to park it to the side instead, in case they needed to get away quickly.

Joe glanced across the group; aside from a strange tension that had developed between Helena, Esther and Justin, as a whole they had fallen into an easy companionship. The loss of family and friends was still sharp, but whatever held them together seemed to ease the grief somewhat.

'If I had access to my lab, I'd be able to see what the virus actually did to her,' Helena muttered that evening, her eyes darting to where Esther slept. She and Joe sipped their coffee around the small fire, trying to stay awake for their watch. She cradled her pistol on her lap. Even when not on watch, the gun she had taken from the pier was always close by. It was more of a comfort now; she rarely used it. They were running low on ammo, even with what Nathan and Georgia had managed to bring.

'What it did?' Joe asked, resting the warm cup on his knee. 'You're a doctor, shouldn't you *know* … Whatever it is?'

Helena scowled into the coals. 'Ignoring the stupidity of that statement for a moment, something this new? Even if we knew what it was, it's impossible to foresee every potentiality. Good or bad,' she mumbled. 'Regardless, I'm a scient … lab tech, not a doctor. For all we know, she's a liability.' She tipped the dregs of her coffee onto the ground.

Joe took another sip of his coffee, wincing at the bitter taste. 'What exactly are you saying? Are you suggesting we kick her out of the group?' He kept his voice low, not wanting it to carry to restless ears in the tents around them. Helena heaved a sigh.

'I … No. Nothing really.' Helena sighed. 'I'm not suggesting anything.' She scowled, looking into her empty mug. 'I guess I just needed to voice my thoughts since I can't bounce theories off my colleagues.'

The dying fire snapped in the silence. Joe looked across at Helena; she had withdrawn into herself again, her brown calculating eyes staring at the dancing flames. His gaze drifted up, following a shadow as it ghosted along the side of the campervan. A soft light flickered in the window of the door, signalling Alex's continued vigil.

Alex had distanced himself from everyone, choosing to pour his attention over the maps they had brought, looking for a way to follow Sarah's initial plan of getting their group safely to the dingo fence. He had decided to make that his homage to her.

The table was completely hidden by the piles of papers he pawed through. The side window was obscured with a touring map that had thick black crosses over where Geelong and Melbourne had once proudly sat along the picturesque bay. A heavy red line ran along what they thought was the length of the dingo fence, with several routes marked in from where they camped now.

Andrew and Tracey had claimed the four-wheel-drive. In spite of the attempts made by others in the group, Tracey and Andrew kept themselves separated for the most part, along with Mick. They preferred to stay in the four-wheel-drive even when the others crowded around the tiny fire in the evenings.

Seth stirred from the patch of earth he had claimed beneath the tarp, hobbling over to join Helena and Joe at the fire, resting against the log that Helena sat on. His leg was doing better, though he had kept the splint on at Helena's instruction.

'Trouble sleeping?' Helena asked softly.

Seth shrugged. 'It was either stare stupidly at the roof, or join you guys. My watch starts soon anyway.' He leaned forward, picking up the coffee pot and swilling it around with a frown. 'It looks like we'll have to go around Ballarat; it's bound to be swamped now.' He leant back to look at Joe. 'I don't suppose you know this area well?'

Joe shook his head. 'I know that the streets were designed by a drunken miner back in the Gold Rush days.' He laughed. 'I think the roads in general lead *to* the city though, not around it. Maybe Alex has a more detailed map of the area somewhere in that pile of his?' he suggested.

Seth nodded. 'I'll go see. In the meantime, get some rest. It's my watch now.'

'Hmm, sleep sounds heavenly,' Helena moaned, slipping down

from the log and stretching. 'The coffee's shit, but there's a cup left in the pot if you hate your liver.' She handed the chipped mug she had been using to him.

He took it with a grimace. 'It looks strong enough to dissolve a spoon.' He turned to watch as they slipped into the flimsy tents pitched between the vans and the fire. Seth poured the last of the muddy brown liquid into the cup and sipped, pulling a face at the taste.

A faint rustling from beyond the tarp wall caught his attention, making Helena and Joe freeze in place. Seth grabbed for his knife, covering the gap between the fire and the tarp in a single, awkward step. He flicked the side up to peer out into the thick darkness.

A white shape loomed out of the dark to his right. He brought the knife down in an arc, aimed at the head of the still formless shape.

'Hey! Woah!' An arm came up to block the strike along with the panicked gasp, and Seth changed the angle of his swing enough to sweep it to his side instead of burying it in the person's skull.

'Justin?' he hissed. 'What the hell?'

'I guess Joe forgot to tell you that I slipped out to spend a penny?'

'I guess he did.' He glanced over at a sheepish-looking Joe.

'Sorry,' Joe mumbled, turning to follow Helena's already retreating form.

Seth exhaled heavily, moving back to the log he had been sitting on.

Justin followed him over, taking the seat that Joe had vacated. He picked up a small branch from the ground between his feet, idly twirling it between his fingers. 'How long can we keep this up?' He didn't lift his eyes from the ground as he spoke.

'What do you mean?' Seth asked.

'Sarah is gone. People aren't going to want to keep following the half-formed plans of a dead girl just because Alex wants to "honour her memory". They're going to want safety, to stay in one spot. We haven't heard anything else from these "other people", nothing about what the government is doing. There hasn't been so much as a squawk on the radio!' He dropped the twig and looked towards the four-wheel-drive. 'Frankly I'm surprised we're all still here.' Justin had made no secret of his distrust of Tracey and her family; it was the worst kept secret in the group, after his dislike of Helena and Esther.

Seth had kept his own doubts to himself, not wanting to add to the growing tension that buzzed through the camp.

'Things are about to change,' Justin murmured, leaning back against the log and shutting his eyes.

'You're not on watch, mate. Wouldn't you rather catch what sleep you can?'

'The nights aren't likely to stay this nice. I'll enjoy it while I can.'

Seth stared at the fire as Justin dozed. No longer the silent, sometimes twitchy man Seth had met, Justin had started to relax and at times could be good company when he wasn't trading barbs with the lab tech. Every now and then, though, Seth thought he saw something dark flash through his eyes, particularly when his gaze fell on Esther or Helena.

His attention drifted over to the dozing man, snorting a laugh when his stomach let out a large growl. Even with Joe's hunting, there wasn't enough to feed everybody adequately, and their supplies were running low. Silently he climbed to his feet. Direction of travel aside, they would have to organise a run into Ballarat, a city that was as large as Geelong, and no doubt just as dead.

He knocked softly on the campervan door, waiting for Alex's muffled 'Enter' before stepping into the dim interior.

'Seth. What can I do for you?' Alex turned on his chair, keeping his voice low so as not to disturb the rest of his family. Anica slept on the edge of the foam bed, Rebecca on the other side. Charlie snuggled close to her mother in the middle. James had curled up on the narrow bench opposite his chair, the covered table between them.

'I'm not surprised to see you still awake,' Seth whispered, leaning against the wall. While his leg had improved to the point where he could move easier, he still tired quickly.

'Sleep … is not easy,' Alex replied. The dramatic shadows cast by the candle over his desk highlighted his gaunt face and deepened the shadows below his eyes. He turned back to the map that lay sprawled across his table. Seth shuffled uncomfortably where he stood, lost for words that were adequate for comforting the stoic man. Maps were piled up on the table, mostly regional or national.

'What are the chances you have a map for Ballarat buried in there?'

'Nil, I'm afraid. I've been trying to piece one together from the larger ones I have. But as it is I can't tell you what roads are most likely blocked or in areas likely to be overrun.' He pinched the bridge of his nose tiredly.

'You look like you need a drink. I'd offer to buy you one, but I'm pretty sure the pubs aren't open,' he offered weakly.

Alex looked up at him again. 'I could go for a drink.' He sighed heavily. 'There's a place just a short way up the road, outside the city limits. Being on the outskirts of the town, they're likely to have a map of sorts too,' he mused, standing up.

'I can't leave the camp without a watch!'

'James can pretend to sleep outside. He's rubbish at it here. Plus, I need a break before I start hallucinating contour lines on every rock.'

James cracked open an eye and scowled at his father. 'Maybe it's because you read too loudly.' The young man stretched, sitting up straight with an audible crack. 'Is there any "coffee" left out there?' He crooked his fingers around the word, as if his disdain of the powdered drink was less than obvious.

'Not in the billie. Is there any left in here?' Seth glanced at Alex, who nodded.

'A little, not much. We'll, see what we can scrounge up while we're out.'

Seth hopped down the single step and hobbled to the campfire, Alex and James following. James tugged the light blanket around his shoulders.

Alex paused, looking around the makeshift camp. 'It's a little far to walk, especially with your leg, and we can't take the cars we have here.'

'Transport's not a problem,' James scoffed. 'We passed a few abandoned cars just up the road. One of them will be sure to have keys still.' He sat on the log, poking a stick into the fire and stirring the coals, sending a flurry of sparks into the dark sky. 'Well, have fun.'

Alex nodded to him, pulling a long-handled axe from behind the door of the camper. Seth patted his pocket, feeling for the reassuring weight of his knife. Alex swept the tarp aside to walk through.

Seth looked back at James. 'You'll be right?'

'I'm good.' He nodded.

Seth returned the gesture, following Alex into the dark.

James breathed in slow and deep. The air still carried the smell of damp earth, spiced with the smoke from their campfire. The slight tang of ozone hinted at more rain to come, something he was sincerely hoping for. He tipped his head back, looking up to the dark sky. The Southern Cross sat almost directly above him, occasionally obscured by an upward flurry of sparks as a blackened log resettled in the pile.

'If we have to run for our lives, I'm glad we can do it in this weather,' Justin spoke up suddenly beside him.

'Mmm, as flee for your life adventures go, this is definitely in my top ten.' He threw the stick into the fire, watching the resultant sparks until they vanished. 'Do you think they'll be all right?'

'Alex and Seth?' Justin turned to look at the young man. 'As long as they find some transport and don't take stupid risks, they'll be fine.' He turned back, relaxing into the silence again. 'Reckon your dad needs the break, or he's going to go mad.' He coughed, pulled the tarp aside slightly and spat into the dark. James scowled in distaste, eliciting a shrug from the man beside him. 'I think it's the smoke. Need to get it out somewhere.'

The faint clunk of gravel-filled Coke cans broke through the night. Both men jerked to attention.

'Could it be them?' James asked.

'They know where the perimeter rope is, and they wouldn't set it off. Douse the fire.'

James jumped to his feet, kicking a small pile of dirt over the low fire. In the sudden darkness, everything took on a menacing feel, the remnants of the smoky haze creating a surreal blanket that curled through the confined space.

'Wake the girls,' Justin hissed. 'Quickly!'

James darted over to the sleeping forms, shaking them sharply. They snapped into a seated crouch, Helena already reaching for her pistol. James held a finger to his lips, unable to see their faces in the dark. Karen was already climbing to her feet when he turned to the campervan.

Justin had moved to the back door of the Bushmaster, risking a peep around the tarp before opening the rear door. He turned to the two women now standing behind him, and held up three fingers before moving his hands apart to indicate they were still a distance off. He then slipped into the warm interior of the truck.

James walked quickly to the campervan to wake his family, leaving Helena to wake up Nathan and Georgia. Three of the infected should be easy enough to take out; they had certainly faced that many before with few problems.

He had just rested his hand on the lump of blankets that covered his wife when the first rasping snarl rattled through the thin windows. Rebecca jerked upright, narrowly missing James's head as she did so. She fumbled to find Charlie, who was starting to fuss. A solid thump on the outside of the truck had her jumping, just barely holding back a squeal.

'What's that? Is that Dad? Where's your dad?' The words slipped out in a half-awake, barely recognisable tumble. Another thump had James pulling Rebecca up from the bed.

'It's not Dad, it's nobody from the group. It's coming from outside.' He picked up Charlie, pressing her into Rebecca's arms. 'There's three infected out the front, there must have been another one behind us.' James could feel his heart thumping wildly in his chest, and he fought to bring it under control as he grabbed for the crowbar by the bed. Woken by the fuss, Anica sat up groggily, fighting the pull of sleep as she took in what was happening. She slid quietly to her feet.

'Four?' Rebecca asked.

'At least. It's too dark to tell for sure.' He kept his voice just under a whisper, trying to track the noises outside. 'We heard the perimeter cans first, Justin saw three out the front. This one makes four.'

Anica stepped out of the campervan. James paused to kiss his wife before stepping down to join her. Rebecca stood in the doorway, holding Charlie tightly before closing the door securely between them and watching from the window.

Joe rubbed his free hand across his scruffy, unkempt stubble. Even freshly dragged from too little sleep, his eyes shone with the same ice blue clarity they held every time he picked up his bow. The boys stood close to him, each nervously twisting what they had grabbed to arm themselves.

Andrew had climbed down from the four-wheel-drive and stood behind them, cricket bat swinging in his hands. Tracey's face was the picture of panic as he herded them towards the campervan. She carried no weapon; she never did, opting instead to hide behind Andrew's solid form, holding his shirt tightly. They all looked to Joe, who looked back at the frightened group as he opened the camper door.

'Mick, go into the campervan with Rebecca and Charlie. She can stay and look after you and Charlie in here. Tracey …'

'I'll stay,' Tracey interrupted with surprising force, guiding her son up the two steps. Joe raised an eyebrow. 'I can't shoot, I can't fight. Rebecca would be more useful out here,' she insisted, reaching to take Charlie from a clearly reluctant Rebecca. The protective mother scowled, her arms tightening slightly around her daughter before placing her on the bed. She leaned down to whisper something in the infant's ear and stood once more, moving to the door.

Joe scowled, his gut insisting that something was off with her uncharacteristic outspokenness. Andrew too was quiet, his eyes locked on the bat in his hands, but they were running out of time. He caught Karen's eye and gestured for her to stay close to the camper, just in case. The growls became louder as the things on the other side grew closer to the tarp stretched over the front. Joe's hands formed fists at his side as he reluctantly agreed, only reassured by Karen slipping subtly towards the rear of the van.

'Helena, can you sit up on the Bushmaster above the twins? If things are too bad we'll need your gun. You can jump through the roof if things get too hairy.'

She nodded, heading over to the truck with the boys. She clambered up the ladder as the twins positioned themselves on either side of the tarp.

'Sam, can you go with Anica out the front? Rebecca can stay inside the tarp in case something gets through. Nathan and Georgia, if you can move behind the Bushmaster, I'll go to the other side with James while Andrew repositions the four-wheel-drive.' He looked at the short woman who held the gun awkwardly and hid his grimace. 'Hopefully it's just the four of them. Don't take unnecessary risks; we just want to clear the area enough to pull the four-wheel-drive around in front of the tarp. It should keep them at bay till we see the signal from Alex and Seth, and we can move on.'

They had prepared for every situation they could think of: the rope they had set up in a ten-metre perimeter with the Coke cans had been Helena's idea, to give them warning of people, or *other things*, approaching. They had also made it clear among the group that if the fire was doused, anyone not in the camp would move further out and start another fire, hopefully luring any of the infected away from the camp to the new distraction, before making their way to the road where the others would meet them. This was the first time the plan had been put into action, and the tension was palpable.

'Okay, let's go.' Joe lifted the bow from its stand and clipped the quiver to his belt.

Notching an arrow loosely, he led the small group out, shifting the tarp to the side just enough to allow them out, then dropping it again. He could see the shadow on the Bushmaster's roof above them as Helena peered into the dark. They broke off to their chosen sides, moving slowly as the shadows took on lives of their own.

A short, sharp whistle split the air from the Bushmaster's roof. Joe turned just as the first infected creature came limping towards them. A child, no more than five years old, lurched in their direction. A tattered, leashed backpack hung from her shoulders, a yellow-haired doll dangled perilously from the opening. As she caught sight of them and stumbled forward, her feet faltered under her tiny body. Joe raised the bow, notching an arrow in its rest.

'Not a child anymore,' he whispered, mentally giving himself permission to shoot. He centred the line of shaft between the tiny blond curls and loosed. He didn't pause to follow the flight of the arrow; instead he reached for the next one. He notched another, hearing solid thumps along the side of the truck. Three more lumbering shadows tore their way through the trees. A young man in torn-off shorts and a tank top covered the ground quickly, soon falling by the next arrow to fly from the bow. Joe dropped the bow as the other two closed the distance, too close for the ranged weapon. A hunched older woman in a stained housedress and a bespectacled man in blood-soaked chef whites reached out for them. Joe raised a short knife and buried it into the forehead of the woman, barely sparing a glance to her collapsed form as he moved onto the next.

James swung the crowbar in his hand forcefully into the head of the shorts-clad man, and without a pause he then swung out at the chef, dropping him quickly. 'Oh shit,' he murmured. One by one, more appeared from between the trees.

Nathan gave a hoarse yell from the side of the truck. Joe could see their dim forms edging towards him as his friends were pushed back by the press of the dead. Rebecca and Anica were next to re-join them, gasping for breath as they ran back to them.

'Get to the trucks! Move the four-wheel-drive in front to block them off,' Joe barked at Andrew, eyeing the dreadful group as they closed in. He yanked the tarp down as they retreated to the campsite.

'There's too many,' James panted. 'We have to move on and try to meet Dad and Seth closer to the road.'

Andrew turned the car on, while Joe herded the small group further in to give him room to shift the car across and block them off properly as they had planned.

'What's he doing?' Rebecca squeaked as she looked at the truck. Andrew hadn't moved the car, looking at them with something akin to guilt clouding his face. Joe frowned and stepped towards him, when two shadows rushed from behind the campervan towards the four-wheel-drive. He made to shout a warning but stopped, recognising Tracey's slim figure pulling at Mick's hand.

'Where are they going?' James made to run towards them.

Tracey threw the door open and hauled her son into the back.

'Charlie!' Rebecca cried, running to the campervan and flying inside.

'James! We need help!' Joe called out from where he was ripping the tarps off the last two cars. James stopped; Joe could see him looking uncertainly over to where Andrew had thrown the car into gear and peeled out. The car bounced over the body of a girl in a floral jumper and sped away, leaving only twin red points of light behind them.

'Dammit! We can't wait! Get to the trucks, we have to go!' Joe pushed Anica to the campervan.

She spun in his grip. 'Where's Alex?' she asked, panicked.

'With Seth. Went to get maps. Go!'

The scattered line of tattered creatures were barely a metre from the camp border now. James ran to the campervan where Anica had settled behind the wheel and had the huge truck idling. Rebecca was kneeling on the bed, closing the rear doors, Karen lay unconscious on the wide bed.

'She left them wide open!' Rebecca's disgust was clear. Pushing at the doors to make sure they were secure, she picked up Charlie and buckled herself into the passenger seat.

Anica had no idea how she had managed to get the truck in gear and ready to move. The last ten minutes were a total blur. James slammed the campervan door shut as the first slaps of flesh against tin echoed through the truck.

'Drive, Mum!' he yelled.

Anica shoved her foot down on the pedal, spinning the tires for a moment before the rubber picked up traction from the packed earth beneath it and the heavy campervan lurched forward. The Bushmaster had already gained ground, pushing through tree branches where they scratched down the sides. Anica followed the red lights ahead, squinting into the dark. She hadn't put her own headlights on, not wanting to give too much light to the predators following behind them. She winced at each pothole and hidden rock as they drove blindly ahead.

She glanced back in the mirror. Rebecca's face was white. Charlie, held tight to her chest, whimpered at each sudden jolt that rocked the van. James had moved to the front of the van again, but beyond him, through the rear window, Anica could see the shadowy forms being left behind and swallowed up by the trees.

The truck in front of them pressed on the breaks, lighting up the road in front with an eerie red. Anica pulled in behind them, keeping her seatbelt fastened as James swung the door open and walked to the rear of the Bushmaster.

Rebecca unsnapped her belt and moved awkwardly to the rear seats, settling into the corner of the cheap foam couch to feed her fussy daughter. Anica watched her for a while, fingers still curled tightly around the steering wheel before her eyes drifted down to her arm. Blood dripped slowly from the crook of her elbow, dribbling down from a scratch on her wrist. She hadn't thought it had been that close, its yellowed teeth catching her flesh before she could wrench it out of range. It wasn't a perfect bite wound, only the slight parting of skin where the jagged corner of a tooth caught her, but already the skin was reddening around the edges and she could feel the heat spreading up her arm. She startled as the door creaked open and James climbed into the empty seat beside her.

'Joe said there's only one place they would have gone near … What happened to you?' He eyed the torn skin that she had tried to conceal with her sleeve.

'I swung my knife a little too wildly. Lesson learned.' She grinned easily at her son, hoping that he wouldn't hear the catch she felt in her throat. James shuffled to the rear of the truck, returning with one of the remaining first-aid packs stashed in the van. He wrapped a bandage firmly around her wrist.

'Do we need to keep you away from sharp objects now?' he muttered lightly, securing it in place with a small safety pin.

'What did Joe say?' she asked, eager to change the subject.

'The pub is about a kilometre down the road. Well, not pub exactly, it's more of a general store. It's closer than the hotel that Dad was talking about. Joe's pretty sure they would have gone there. If we keep to the road, we'll get to it quickly or pass them on the way back if we're lucky.'

'Are you okay?' Rebecca called from the back. 'Do you want me to drive?'

'That might be for the best.' Anica smiled back, holding her hands out as Rebecca stood with Charlie. 'Would you mind if I held her for a while?'

Rebecca nodded, handing the squirming toddler to her grandmother before sliding into the driver's seat and starting the car.

Alex and Seth had been lucky, stumbling across an abandoned convertible a little further down the road. Choosing to ignore the scattered clothes and blood stained seats, Alex turned the key still inserted in the ignition, smiling as the engine purred to life. A companionable silence filled the car. The silhouetted trees blurred as they gained speed, bracketing the curved road. Alex soon pulled off the road, coasting into the small car park of a general store and turning the car off. The soft ticking of the engine spilled through the warm night.

'She shouldn't have been first.' Alex's chin drooped to his chest as he spoke softly.

Seth remained silent, letting the grieving father voice his thoughts in peace.

'Every time she watched those ridiculous movies, pointing out stupid choices, telling us what they should have done instead … If anyone was supposed to survive this, it should have been her.' He fell quiet, rubbing his hands over his tired eyes.

'Let's find you a drink,' Seth offered, waving at the dark building ahead.

Alex just swung the door open in answer. Seth stabilised his crutch onto the ground and stood unsteadily. They moved cautiously to the front of the store and swung the unlocked door open softly.

Alex pulled his attention back to the room ahead, stepping quietly inside. The sparse shelves had already been emptied of most of their goods and the few liquor shelves the store had behind the counter were dry.

'Water?' Seth offered lamely.

'Water's perfect. We might as well see what else we can find here so it's not a total loss.' Alex flipped through the piles of paper at the front, throwing them back onto the counter when he couldn't find anything useful.

Seth picked gingerly around the broken shelves and stickiness that coated the floor. The musty smell of mould had both men breathing through their mouths.

'Let's try the back rooms before we give up,' Seth murmured. He moved to the small door behind the cashier counter. The till lay broken on the floor, stripped of its notes and coins, a silver puddle of five-cent pieces scattered around.

They found little as they picked through the empty shop; even the store rooms at the back had been emptied by opportunistic scavengers. What remained formed a meagre pile of odds and ends the two men accumulated in the centre of the room.

'It's not much,' Seth said, eyeing the modest stack.

'It's less than that. It's the few things we're *not* running short of, and a poorer quality at that,' Alex grumbled, picking up a length of frayed rope and throwing it back down.

They had managed to find a few cans that had obviously not appealed to those who had come before: a small tin of asparagus, several cans of chickpeas, empty water bottles and several boxes of 'feminine hygiene products', as Alex had delicately stated when he had thrown them into the pile.

'Frankly I'm surprised there's this much left,' Alex said darkly. 'I knew there wouldn't be any booze.' He slumped against the counter then cocked his head, leaping to his feet and ripping a framed picture off the wall. 'At least it's not a total loss!' He held up a black and white map of Ballarat triumphantly and jumped up to sit on the counter.

'Wait, shhh,' Alex hissed. 'Do you hear that?'

Seth tilted his head in the same direction, the faint hum of an engine buzzed through the air. 'Is that … Where is it coming from?' he asked, hobbling towards the door. The buzz grew louder.

Alex made it to the door first, Seth manoeuvring his bulky leg brace through skewed and up-ended shelves. Alex pushed the door open, standing still, gesturing for Seth to do the same.

'I'm not sure; it sounds like it's coming from everywhere at once.'

'Maybe it's echoing off the trees,' Seth suggested. The hum sounded close now, and a soft light highlighted the trees leading away from the gold mining town.

'It's from the camp, something's happened!' Alex ran to the side of the road, facing away from the city. The spill of yellow light grew stronger as the headlights rounded the corner. He stepped into the centre of the road and waved his arms.

The heavy Bushmaster slowed and veered towards them, pulling in alongside the building till it was hidden by the shadows. With a whine of breaks the campervan coasted to a stop in front of the small shop. Karen stirred, clutching at her head as she fought the dizziness that made her sway.

Anica threw open the driver's door and fell into Alex's arms, pressing her head into his neck. He struggled to hold her upright as he looked quizzically at his son.

'What happened?'

'The camp was swarmed, we had to get out. It was lucky we managed to find you.' Rebecca reached down to turn the campervan off, but the hum of engines still cut through the group.

'Joe, turn it off,' Seth called.

'It is off, it's not us,' he replied softly.

'Maybe Tracey's coming back?' Karen asked with a scowl, walking to the centre of the road.

'Back?' Alex looked around, noticing the missing car for the first time. 'Where did she go? Where's Andrew and Mick?'

'They left when we had to break camp. They pissed off.' Joe was angry, not bothering to hide it.

'So, is it them?'

'I doubt it. They went in the other direction, and that doesn't sound like a four-wheel-drive.'

'No,' Sam cut in, 'it's higher pitched, like …'

'Motorbikes,' James muttered, frightened eyes coming to rest on his wife and daughter. Mental images of the frenzy gang he had seen with Sarah on day one became superimposed over the shadows of the trees hiding the oncoming vehicles from sight.

Chapter Three
A City Divided

Dr Marcus paced the length of the room, his fists clenched at his side a clear sign of his agitation. His entire working life had revolved around the study of disease treatment, hoping to find that one breakthrough where his name would go down in history. *His* studies, *his* findings, reviewed and referenced worldwide. His own golden apple to ensure his immortality. Now, in the hour that he should be accepting the accolades of his peers, some halfwit monkey in a spacesuit throws a bloody tractor in the mix, effectively rendering *years* of research useless!

Well ... almost useless.

He stopped by a steel table in the middle of the room he had laid claim to within the genetics lab of Melbourne University. It was empty for the moment, freshly cleaned after he had finished with his latest examination. The irate doctor walked to the window and looked outside. The once busy city streets were just visible through a gap between the buildings.

The web of tramlines had been eerily quiet along Royal Parade for the past few weeks; crowded footpaths now blocked by a very different type of pedestrian. Beyond the road, he could see the roofline of the hospital that had ejected him from their uneducated ranks. The first weeks had seen him reduced to hiding in filthy, urine-soaked stairways. Nothing but a door between him and the hungry throng outside.

It had been pure providence to find the partially open window into the lower floor of the university. The simple-minded tunnel-dwelling refugees who had the nerve to judge his work as 'immoral' and cast him to the outside world had closed off the underground section between the huge complexes. They had shown remarkable stupidity in their inability to recognise the necessity of research in this new age. This was the age of science. Perhaps he could expect no more from secretaries and salespeople. Especially since they couldn't recognise the superior intellect within their own group. Since their numbers had reduced to the point where it was deemed an unnecessary risk, they had erected makeshift barriers to contain their claimed area to a manageable space.

He smirked unpleasantly, who was he to say no to such an opportunity?

He had broken through their barrier easily, replacing it with his own, easily accessible one. The new entry was covered with a heavy tarp that hid it from the little used tunnel, allowing him easy access through which he could keep an eye on certain individuals in the mismatched group.

They had changed little, turning their chosen area into something that resembled a large, comfortable bunker, blocking off all but two entrances to create a large safe room they could retreat to if necessary. He had watched with interest as the crowded area, home to their attempt at mental health care, was slowly emptied of its occupants into the larger group as the odd nature of the virus on the schizophrenic patients was unveiled.

The exiled doctor waited.

He had kept to the shadows, acting only as an observer while

he readied his area for work. He had dragged cages from the zool-
ogy building, and set up a small desk in front of the window. He
had also collected trays of medical equipment from the student
labs. Most important had been the radio he had stolen from the
refugees' communications room.

That had been fortuitous. Once again he was in contact with
his central base, and through them his one remaining colleague
from the Geelong labs. It had been a relief to know she had not
only escaped, but also now held company with two viable subjects
of the primary virus. Even limited to sporadic communications,
they were able to pass on what they observed from both stations
and relay that back to their superiors, who would be working
blind without their contributions. Now he only had to wait for
more of his own subjects to continue the more *comprehensive* and
less open side of their research.

He got the chance he had been waiting for five days after he
had prepared his rooms in the university.

Patient 61, the woman he had been observing since she had
bitten and subsequently infected an orderly, was one of the newer
additions to the scavenging crew. He knew she had shown no signs
of turning in spite of the bite that still scarred her skin, and he was
sure she held the answers he was looking for in her rewired brain.

Dr Marcus had watched as she, like the other prior patients,
had been integrated into one of the many teams. On their return,
a little over a week since his ousting, he was given his chance.

The ragtag group of tunnel dwellers had grown complacent in
their own environment. The few evacuated patients and the staff
who had survived were not seasoned survivalists, something he
took full advantage of.

They walked quickly through the tunnels, preferring speed to quiet, each carrying what they could. He had noticed the supplies they brought back seemed to shrink in quantity each time they went out, driving them to further and further targets. He kept his own footsteps light as he followed them. The blonde was slower than the others, falling a few steps behind the group as they hurried back to their families. Dr Marcus increased his pace slightly as the last of the group rounded the corner, blocking them from view.

Like prey recognising the approach of its predator, the blonde froze. The doctor saw her start to turn around and he closed the narrow space between them. Wrapping his arm around her neck, he choked off her muffled scream. His fingers dug into her soft skin, feeling her frenzied movements slow as he starved her valuable brain of oxygen.

She slumped, senseless in his arms. Sweeping an arm under her knees, he retraced his steps up the tunnel to his hidden door, nudging the heavy tarp aside. The drapery fell back into place behind him as he went back to the university.

Peta came back to her senses slowly, fighting the nausea and blinding headache that beat against her skull. She could smell the thick metallic scent of blood, something they had all grown somewhat accustomed to over the last weeks.

She cracked an eyelid, the piercing light wrenching a groan from her as she closed it tightly once more, blocking out the sun.

'Welcome back. For a little bit I thought the treatment might finish the job without giving me the opportunity to check my own hypothesis.'

The voice was calm and measured, every inch the professional. She opened her eyes, keeping them at a squint to block most of the offending glare. Through her lashes, she could see thick bars separating her from the rest of the room.

A well-lit steel table took up a place of prominence, its shiny top reflecting the sun throughout. A plain desk sat to the side of the window, with a steel trolley almost blocking the mattress that peeked out from behind it. From where she was sprawled on the ground, she couldn't see what was on top of the table, but the red drips that trailed like honey down the side hinted at nothing good.

She could see the hunched form of a man seated at the desk, staring through a microscope. A small vial of what could be blood sat in a stand on the desk beside him. He turned slightly to face her, his features hidden by the window's glare behind him.

'What is this? What are you doing?' she asked, her voice rough and slurred, her throat dry.

'This?' He turned back to the desk in front of him, extending his arms as though to embrace the structure. 'This is progress.' He pushed his chair back and stood. Grinning coldly, he walked towards her till he stood in front of the bars, peering into her eyes earnestly. 'You should be proud, you're on the front line of a huge scientific breakthrough.' He looked beside her; unbidden her eyes followed. Another cage sat beside her, and another beyond that. In the cage immediately to her left, the floor was coated in blood. Remnants of tissue and bone shards littered the carpet. She paled, closing her eyed against the rush of nausea. The doctor tutted condescendingly.

'Each stage of medical advancement inevitably incurs its casualties.' His tone was still passive, devoid of emotion. 'If it makes you feel any better, it looks like you won't undergo the same process. You seem to be completely immune to the virus. Though I was a little surprised that even the tissue donation had so few ill effects.' She looked up at him in horror, then down to what she suddenly realised was not a stiff arm, but a heavily bandaged one.

'You're mad!' she hissed, terror and anger warring for prevalence as she found her voice.

Unfazed by her horror, the doctor smiled, almost kindly. 'Many great minds have been considered mad, you know. Galileo was labelled a heretic.'

'They didn't have to kill people to change the world.' Her jaw clenched and she turned to face the corner of the room, unable to look at him as she spoke.

'How many people do you think died for the advances we have in cardiac treatment?' He appeared distracted, as though already dismissing her from his mind.

'I'm sure Mengele said the same thing. *Hero* is not a term associated with his name among acceptable circles,' she said. She stopped herself before continuing, trying to centre her thoughts, looking for a way out. 'I assume I'm here because I was bitten and didn't turn?' She jerked her head at the mess beside her. 'What about him?'

He glanced disinterestedly at the bloody remains. 'The results of an earlier test.' He sucked air through his teeth. 'It was … unsuccessful.' Peta cringed, now trying desperately not to picture flesh-eating rats. 'Don't worry, I have high hopes for you. You've already passed the preliminary testing stage, and your lab results are looking good. You still have higher than normal levels of leukocytes in your system and your blood and hormones are already changing. The virus is … different, cleaner in your system than it was in his. I can work with this one.'

The doctor was silent for a moment, his eyes distant, calculating. Peta felt like he had forgotten about her presence completely, so absorbed in his own inner dialogue that his words were more to himself than any real attempt to hold a conversation.

'We're so close to finishing what we started. We won't lose this project, not when we've been given *such* an opportunity. We're going to be the toast of the community when we leave here.'

Peta got the distinct impression that 'we' did not include 'she'. She paled and closed her eyes against his excitement.

'And you!' He turned his attention fully onto her. 'You don't even know what you've been given. What this can do. *This* can change the world! The virus is one thing, but you changed the virus! You're *beyond* human now.' Unable to take more of his delusional ranting she covered her face and screamed.

'You *sick fuck*. You're experimenting on survivors! Are you so twisted that you can only see people as glorified lab rats?'

His mouth stretched into a thin, wan smile and he turned away from her, facing the shiny table in the centre of the room.

'Do you even know my name?' she sobbed, suddenly needing to be seen as more than just samples, or impersonal data. 'It's Peta, Peta Richards. I h—'

He cut her off before she could continue. 'That doesn't matter anymore! It has no bearing on what you are now. You are here because of *this*.' He held up the red vial that had rested on his desk. 'Your blood, your *brain*, holds the key to the future. This is a new breed of humanity. A *stronger* breed. You're beyond disease.'

Her hand drifted up to the bandage in shock. Fingers pulled at the gauze, pushing it down to reveal track marks underneath alongside a darker patch of skin that looked foreign, as though it had been fused to her own arm.

'What did you do?' she demanded, pulling the bandage off completely. 'What did you give me?'

'Everything! Nothing has stuck!' His enthusiasm was almost maniacal. She pushed back against the wall. 'From the common cold to Lupus! It's amazing what you can actually find in a hospital lab. Mind you, I was a little surprised that it didn't translate into a vaccine.' He glanced contemptuously at the caged corpse. 'Maybe on the next one.' His excitement trailed into a musing hum as he stalked back to the desk, picking up a notebook and flipping through it.

'You would sacrifice a country for *this*? You won't get away with this,' she cried after him.

He scoffed, lowering himself into the desk chair and leaning back. 'Sacrifice? I'm saving this country!' He didn't wait for her answer, leaning forward eagerly to share. 'You *have* turned, you know. You're really not human anymore.'

Peta looked up, shocked. He had mentioned this already, but this time it took on a gravity that sunk the words into her brain.

'Sure, you don't *look* like them, as far as I can tell. You don't share their simpleminded drive to bite and infect. You can reason and talk like anyone else. Make no mistake though, blood doesn't lie. You are one of them, and not even the reintroduction of any kind of infected blood seems to change that.' He leaned forward as though passing on a confidence. 'It doesn't even have to be a match!'

A squawk came from a small box on the desk. He picked up a handpiece and depressed the button.

'This is Melbourne.' He released it and there was silence before a static rich voice came back.

'I don't have long. Have you acquired the subject you mentioned?'

He didn't spare her a glance as he replied. 'Acquired and secured. Preliminary tests have shown the virus is pure and active. Viral loading is exactly the same as a fully infected patient within the host body. Subject seems impervious to all introduced pathogens or contraindicated additives. Have you seen anything on your side?'

'No visible changes yet. I don't have access to the materials you do at the moment. I have managed to observe the introduction of the infection into a clean host with good effect. I will be in touch when I'm situated to begin the next phase. Have you been in contact with central?'

'Contact has been made. Will you be retreating south for the extraction?'

'About to start moving shortly.' The female voice was interrupted by faint shouting.

'Helena!' he called, showing what looked like true concern for the first time since Peta had woken. 'Are you there?'

'Shit. Hit a snag. I'm going to have to pull back. I'll be in contact when I can.'

The box fell silent. Slowly, he replaced the handset, pulling another notebook out and writing furiously before placing the book into the drawer and walking out of the room, grumbling under his breath.

Peta watched as the doctor left the room. Waiting a minute till she was sure he was actually gone, she pulled herself up shakily, kneeling in the confined space as her hands gripped the bars tightly for balance. Darting nervous looks towards the door, she ran her hands over every inch of the cage, looking for something that might offer a way out. Aside from a small slide up portion that was far too small for her frame, the bars were solid and welded into the metal base beneath her.

Peta was exhausted; her fruitless pushing and pulling at the unyielding bars offered nothing but exhaustion and frustration. She slumped against the bars behind her, keening softly in her despair.

Heavy footsteps pulled her from her dark thoughts and she scurried backwards as the door was violently kicked in. The doctor stalked in with a young man she didn't recognise slung over his shoulder. He was securely tied from neck to knees, a cloth tied over his face. He hefted him onto the cold surface of the metal table with a grunt.

Peta watched, unable to look away.

The doctor's tall form stood between her and the still figure, almost blocking her line of sight completely. The glint of sunlight danced off the edge of the scalpel as he lifted it from the trolley and opened the boy's forehead with deft fingers. Her skin prickled with heat. She swallowed the saliva that pooled in her throat till it proved too much and she emptied what little was in her stomach onto the floor of her cage. Her ears buzzed with white noise, turning into a whining, metallic shriek that scraped at her nerves.

The bone saw cut easily into the skull, the top falling onto the table with a sickening clunk as he finished. Distracted as she was by the high definition horror show before her, she almost missed when he spoke to her once more, his voice showing no more emotion than a bored lecturer before his students.

'A fully infected brain has no reaction to medications or introduction of pathogens at all. Sedation has no effect, making restraints necessary. Typical antipsychotic medications seemed to show some improvement for a while; however, this has not been effective beyond ten minutes in any subject.' As he spoke, he lifted the brain from its bone casing and placed it gently on the trolley.

'Are you going to kill me too?' she asked quietly.

He didn't even afford her a glance as he spoke down to the table. 'I've not yet learned all you have to tell me. I would be a foolish man indeed to throw away such an opportunity.'

Peta buried her head in her arms again, wanting to shut out the words. Her head swum, the shock and fear expounding her exhaustion and overwhelming her senses, finally plunging her into merciful unconsciousness.

Dr Marcus glanced unfeelingly at the senseless girl lying insensate in her own filth, then turned back to the brain on the tray. Gentle fingers prodded at the pink organ, tracing the black veins of necrotic tissue where they weaved through the sulci. He pulled out a large sharp knife, bisecting the brain quickly and lifting one half to examine the walnut-like shape. The black veins reached up from the basal ganglia, leaving its destructive trails through the tissue. He pulled out a notebook, drawing the dead and inflamed tissue that marked the progression of the disease, writing in his neatest hand what he could see. Pushing the book aside, he sliced a thin cross-section from the organ and placed it carefully on a glass slide, preparing it for the microscope and covering it with another slide. Dropping the rest of the brain into a small container that already held formaldehyde, he shifted it back to sit beside a similar dish that held another brain, this one with healthy pink tissue, and no sign of infection or disease.

He pulled out another book and opened it beside the first, a sketch of the healthy brain across the page showed the dramatic decline of the infected person. He glanced back to the cage, to the blonde hair covering the skull that held the final piece of his collection. Once he had that, he wouldn't even need his partners. He would have everything he ever dreamed. He pulled a face at the unpleasant mess left on his workspace. Until he added the last brain to his samples, though, he had work to do.

Chapter Four

The Floating Horror

Jen closed her eyes as she lay back on the hard cot she shared with Daniel. She was alone for now, Daniel having gone to 'do the rounds' as they called it. The group they had come in with had been isolated to their rooms since they had come aboard. They weren't the only refugees on board. The equipment and vehicles had been removed from the bowels of the ship near the beginning of the outbreak to make room, the cavernous space sectioned off with plywood or thin metal sheets to give the illusion of separate rooms.

No one had been allowed up to the soldiers' areas though. All they knew of them was that from the mix of uniforms and accents, the force on board was made up of factions from around the world. This didn't surprise them; it made sense that there would be a worldwide response to the threat posed. The HMAS *Canberra* was still operating from what they could hear, the shouts and noises of drills filtered down into the artificially lit rooms at all hours.

Jen had started to hate the dark and craved the feel of sun on her skin. Even in the confines of the hospital, they had at least seen the sky. Here, they had no idea if they had even moved from the southern coast.

She started as a knock rapped on the thin wall beside the privacy curtain and a trolley was pushed through, not waiting for her permission to enter. Two armed men followed the curtain, letting it waft back into place behind them. Ivazov and Callet, according to the names on their uniforms.

'Jen and Daniel Woodward?' The question wasn't needed; they asked it every time in heavily accented Russian. 'Where is Mr Woodward, ma'am?'

'He's just checking on the group.'

His face tightened into a scowl. 'All civilians are required to be in their rooms for meals.' Ivazov's reminder was terse and sharp, clearly not happy with the breach in protocol.

This was one thing Jen would never get used to: having armed guards deliver their meals.

The curtain swung aside again, allowing Daniel's entrance.

'I'm here. Sophia was feeling a little poorly. The circulated air down here must be passing a bug around.' He moved to the trolley, lifting the lid off the dish. 'Mmm, powdered potato. How did you know?'

The second man glowered at him unamused. 'Be grateful you're getting anything at all. The only reason you're—'

'You be in your rooms for every meal,' Ivazov cut him off, shooting him a sharp look. 'We will have the medics attend your associates. Make sure you are in your quarters for meals, sir.' The words stopped just short of a bark as they left, the curtain swishing closed behind them.

'It's strange. Since we were rescued, I feel less free than when we were hiding under the hospital,' Jen groused. Daniel held a finger to his lips to shush her. It was difficult to realise that though they were now safe, they were at the mercy of such a rigid authority.

'We'll be all right.' Daniel smiled softly. 'Let's just keep our complaints behind curtained doors,' he reminded her, wrapping his fingers gently around her shoulders and pulling her close. 'We'll get through this, the worst is over.'

She sighed, relaxing into his hold. 'I know. I just want to breathe fresh air again.'

'I'll see what I can do. We still haven't heard from Jeffrey. Without knowing what's happening, we're blind.'

Jeffrey, the one member of the HYDRA who had come with the ship-bound group, had been singled out by the lieutenant commander who had been there to welcome them aboard. He had taken Jeffrey to another part of the vessel, and he hadn't been seen since. Six weeks of silence and some were starting to think he was dead, a thought that was not helping the already tense atmosphere in the ship.

They ate in silence. Weeks of pretending to be married had left them feeling like they truly were. He had been half-joking when asked for their status for the register, but her relief at the added layer of security, and seeing how other couples had been separated as they gave their own status, had convinced Daniel to leave it uncorrected. Jen had no regrets about the deception.

Frantic footsteps interrupted their meal and Kylie, one of the survivors they had brought with them, swept breathlessly into the room.

'Sophia is gone!' she panted. 'They took her!'

'What? Kylie, calm down. What happened?' Jen jumped up, pressing her hands to the panicked woman's cheeks, keeping her voice calm.

'They were bringing the food.' Her voice stuttered as she fought to breathe. 'They left the tray and took her!'

Daniel pushed his chair back, pushing the curtain aside as he swept through. Jen grabbed Kylie's hand, dragging her along behind him. The shantytown that had sprung up in the cavernous space was filling quickly as people came out to see what the noise was. One by one, others joined in with their own missing, name after name was called out as people added their own friends and family, removed for medical treatment and not returned.

'What's going on?' Jen could feel her heart begin to race as their numbers swelled. Of the ninety who had come with them to the ship, fifteen had been taken for treatment or further tests—a 'routine health check' the soldiers had assured them. They had known this already, having to comfort confused family members as they did their rounds. Their prolonged absence had been put down to the medics wanting to make sure they were okay; now, with even more names on the list, they were starting to second guess that conclusion.

Strangers joined them now, other groups that had been on board when they had been pulled from the Yarra's mouth, or groups that had joined them afterwards.

'My Kerry wasn't even sick!' one woman called out. 'I'd just gotten her back!'

'Our Don as well,' another said. 'He actually got better! He wasn't hearing the voices anymore!'

Jen slowed, pieces jostling for position in her mind. Most of their own mentally ill people had been left behind under the city. She turned and faced the direction the last call had come from.

'Does anyone here suffer from schizophrenia?' she asked. 'Not those who were taken, people still here?' Silence followed her question, until a woman pushed her way to the front.

'Kerry had it. She was taken a few days after we got here.' The woman's face was lined with stress. 'She got better! She wasn't sick at all! I don't know why they took her.'

'Was she bitten?' Jen asked. The woman paled. 'We saw some of the mentally ill people in our group get better after they were bit,' Jen hastened to explain. 'They all got better, like you said Kerry did.'

The woman nodded hesitantly. 'She was. We didn't know what it was then, but by the time we had figured it out, she had gotten better! Her boyfriend said she wasn't hearing voices anymore. He was taken when he got that bug going around. He wasn't bit though!'

Jen looked around the swollen group, many were nodding. 'So everyone with schizophrenia was taken, then people started getting sick, and *they* were taken too?' she asked.

'How did we miss this?' Jen whispered to Daniel, upset at the picture painted by the distraught crowd.

'We were the only ones who came in a large enough group to notice. Most of these people came alone or with families. Easy to think you're an isolated incident when you have no one to talk to.' Daniel rested his hand on her shoulder.

'What are they doing with them though? It sounds bigger than a normal quarantine.' Jen's eyes were unfocused as she thought over the information they had. 'None of them have come back. Is it because they're still sick? Or …' She spun on her heel, cutting a path to the far door. 'We need to know what they're doing. We need to find Jeffrey.'

Daniel kept pace easily beside her, a solid shadow of support. As they neared the door, the crowd of people trailing them, he held out a hand to grasp her shirt.

'Wait. We don't know how they'll respond to this kind of

accusation. They might have us under close surveillance even now, watching for this exact response.'

'We know they're watching us, we're quarantined.'

'We don't know how closely they're watching us though, or why. I doubt the armed escort with the meals is to keep the mashed potatoes safe, and I think there's more to the main door being locked than just "keeping the civilians safe".'

She paused. 'I thought that was just part of the uniform.'

'They wouldn't have wanted anyone to panic,' he mused, turning to the crowd around them. 'I need you all to stay quiet.' He waited for the rumbles to die down before knocking on the door.

With a bang, the door was pushed inwards, heavy steel meeting Daniel's face with a crunch. Blood sprayed across Jen's face and shirt. She stared slack-jawed as a river of camouflage flooded through into the room. Heavy boots stepped carelessly over Daniel's unresponsive body, blood pooling around his head in a gory halo.

Jen's world became a mess of noise and movement as she watched, hidden behind the door, as their own military pointed rifles at the unarmed crowd. Women screamed, hiding children from the dead stare of the barrels.

Ivazov stepped into the front rank. His voice commanded enough to stun everyone into silence as he barked his command in his stunted English.

The hush that fell was terrifying.

'We are aware that you have questions regarding the whereabouts of your companions.'

It was with great effort that Jen pulled her eyes from the still form of her only source of comfort and onto the wall of soldiers that had mercifully still not noticed her, tucked as she was behind the door.

'I have been asked to inform you that they are in the best of care, and your ongoing quarantine is in place not only for our safety, but yours as well.'

One man hidden in the back was unable to hold back a snort of disbelief. Both Jen and the commanding figure snapped their heads up to search for them. Jen frowned, the new angle placing something in her peripheral vision that she hadn't noticed before. On the ceiling was a small black dome, and another set a short distance away. Her eyes widening, she sought out every camera that had gone unnoticed to this point, strategically placed behind the girders that laced the celling. No wonder they had responded so quickly! They had probably been watching for this unrest for weeks now, watching for anyone showing signs of illness around them. This didn't feel like quarantine. A slight uniformed soldier marched up to Ivazov, passing him a note that he read silently before turning and issuing a few hand signals to those behind him.

With a disbelieving glance at where Daniel still lay, she whispered a silent apology for leaving him, and slipped out the door, letting the strident voice echo behind her.

The small corridor she found herself in was dark and very close. She stretched out her hands to find the walls and felt her way along, away from the line of soldiers. Her fingers found the bottom rung of a ladder just as a shout, a thump and the clear report of gunfire chased her down the hallway. Then a solid boom rocked the ship.

Chapter Five
The Division

The high-pitched hum of motors had every eye turning to the road. Joe scowled, fingering the shaft of an arrow as he shifted a little. Helena pulled the pistol from where she had squirreled it away. Everyone else seemed to tense, their hands moving to rest on the weapons they held. Nathan, Georgia and Seth stood at the front of the group, as Anica herded Rebecca, Charlie and Helena towards the campervan. Esther stepped back, holding the door open for them but, Joe noted, not stepping up to join them inside. Helena looked as though she wanted to protest being closed up away from the action, but James turned pleading eyes on her.

'I would feel better if you were in there with the gun,' he insisted.

She huffed an irritated sigh but moved inside, eyeing Esther carefully.

Joe could understand her confusion; the normally mousy girl would not ordinarily have voluntarily joined the group outside. This bolder, braver girl was something new, the difference already striking despite having known her for so short a time.

He joined the others, and stood beside Alex, who was trying unsuccessfully to push Anica in the direction of the campervan. Giving up, he left her with James and moved next to Nathan and Georgia.

The bright headlights of five motorbikes rounded the trees that hid the road from them, bathing the road in a yellow glare. They slowed to a stand as they approached. One figure swung his leg over the heavy machine and walked towards them, standing a few steps in front of the others. His imposing bulk was easily on par with the military physique of Seth and Nathan, the rest of his features swallowed in his silhouette. A small dog leapt from between two riders behind him, padding forward to stand at his feet. He raised his hand and the motors cut off, plunging the road into an eerie silence.

'Nice bikes,' Seth observed, breaking the silence. 'I can't help but think they might attract a lot of unwanted attention though.'

The man laughed softly, glancing back at his own. 'They serve their purpose. The streets are too crowded for anything bigger.' He nodded meaningfully towards the campervan.

'It serves its purpose,' Seth echoed back.

'Kill the lights, idiots. It's rude to keep another man blinded when you're talking to him,' he shot back over his shoulder. The sudden dark had everyone blinking furiously as they tried to adjust, moving closer together as they unconsciously sought the safety of the group.

Joe eyed the newcomers warily. Despite their imposing stances, and a silence that seemed to simmer with an implied threat, they made no overt move towards them. He handed his bow to Sam, fingering the arrow he had slipped up his sleeve and stood beside Alex.

'What brings you this way?' Alex asked, holding his ground.

The man stepped confidently forward, the soft moonlight not enough to show his face. 'Habit. Safety. We do routine patrols to check how many of the bastards are nearby, where they're headed, gather food, and look for trespassers and so on.' He waved a hand.

Joe frowned at the careful tone. He knew this man, or at least, men like him. They presented a friendly face to the world, but if you knew what to look for they gave themselves away. It was the honey smoothness of their voice, while their eyes were edged with barbed wire. It was the easy way they stood, while their hands twitched for a weapon at their side.

'Does it always take five people to patrol?' Alex asked dubiously.

The man shrugged. 'I never said *we* were the patrol,' he replied, his smooth voice giving nothing away. 'We're the …' He paused as if searching for the words. '… threat assessment for the Ballarat Kings. Our patrol noticed your little camp and we're here to make sure you keep moving on.'

The emphasis on *keep* clearly warned them against any ideas they might have entertained of staying in the Gold Rush city. The small dog stood suddenly, growling softly as he turned to face the rest of the bikers. A young man behind the burley spokesperson restrained the dog and seemed to tense, glancing around him. He raised a hand as though wanting to interrupt, but hesitated.

Alex raised his hands in what he hoped was a light-hearted surrender gesture, trying to diffuse the tense situation, and backed up slightly.

Joe narrowed his eyes; he had heard of the Ballarat Kings and now wanted nothing more than to get their group moving. He could see Seth stiffen at the tone and Nathan and Georgia shifted slightly into a ready stance, taking their prompt from him. Sam, however, seemed to be distracted, eyeing the tree line that held the dog's attention behind the bikes instead of the threat in front of them.

'Sorry, can I ask something really quick?' Sam said nervously.

Joe frowned, glancing at the dog and up into the shadows.

'How many of you are there?' Sam asked.

The stranger mirrored Joe's incredulous look at the seeming non sequitur. 'Five bikes, five riders.'

Joe turned to follow Sam's line of sight, suddenly understanding the question when he saw the extra shadow limping towards them.

'Shit,' the main biker muttered. 'It's time to go, boys!'

A young man staggered forward into the moonlight. His left leg had been shredded, but not enough to stop him walking. He snatched at the arm of a boy in the back who looked to be no older than the twins. The young man screamed and stumbled forward, bringing his small gun up to fire blindly in his panic. The creature's shoulder jerked backwards as one of the bullets tore straight through, his legs twisting beneath him as he fell to the ground, still reaching towards the retreating boy. A tall blond in a biker's vest cried out in pain as a bullet lodged in his arm and he spun on his heels, clutching at the wound.

The man they had been speaking to stalked over to the downed creature still clawing towards the young man, pulling out a large blade as he went. He struck down hard, splitting the skull before wrenching the knife back out and turning to the blond biker. Without missing a beat, he swung again, driving the blade through the top of the man's head. The leather-clad group merely turned away, their blank expressions suggesting that this was not out of the ordinary.

Joe saw Seth stiffen, his soft 'fuck' summing up their combined reactions nicely. Joe grabbed the back of Seth's shirt in one hand, seeing Alex do the same to Nathan and Georgia, and they moved back towards the campervan as a group, already hearing growls from the woods around them.

Sam stumbled, just long enough for the bikers to catch up. The imposing figure turned, pulling a gun from his belt, the rest of the bikers following suit. Joe froze as four muzzles were levelled towards them, one pressed against Sam's head, his eyes wide with fear. Their own group had four guns between them, and three of those were inside the cars.

The mean-looking man addressed Seth. 'Nothing personal, but you just became less of a priority. Get to the campervan!' the biker barked behind him, gesturing his men forward, dragging Sam along with him.

James shot a frightened look towards the van the currently hid his wife and daughter and back to the tree line that seemed to ooze with movement as more of the infected residents made their way out from the shadows.

The biker gang ran to the campervan, pushing James away from the door where he was desperately trying to get in to be with his family. A hard shove had him sprawling to the ground as the black-clad group swarmed into the confined quarters.

Rebecca had been watching out the window, her heart in her throat and Charlie in her arms, as the lead biker had taken out both the infected man and his own man without a hint of remorse. She bounced her daughter softly, sushing her as she started to whimper. She could see James's face, dimly lit by the headlights of the camper. She knew that face well, the fear etched in the clenched jaw was obvious to her, the way his eyes kept darting over to where she was hidden. He had crossed his arms, trying and failing to hide the tension in them. Rebecca paced to the window, humming softly to her daughter. Her hands shook, anxiety plucking at her nerves. Her brain conjured up scenarios, one after another, each one worse than the last. This wasn't going to end well.

Helena had stayed near the door where she could see out the lower window. As the leader started to herd his group towards them, Rebecca snatched the gun from Helena's grasp, shoved Charlie into her arms and crowded her against the table, flinging the cushions to the floor. Helena frowned at her over the squirming child in her arms as Rebecca opened the seat to reveal the cramped cavity beneath, a new strength suffusing her muscles as she made the decision her entire body fought against. Rebecca rested a hand on her daughter's tiny head, levelling a hard look at the short woman.

'If I were your height, I wouldn't hesitate to leave you out here and hide in there with her myself. As this is not the case, I need you to get the hell in.'

Helena stared at her in mute shock as the usually soft motherly tones were hardened to military exactness. Rebecca spoke quickly and sharply, her animated hands pushing one of the cushions down inside to create a soft floor under the seat. They could hear footsteps now, peppered with infrequent stumbles, curses and thuds. James pleaded for them to stop, and Rebecca could hear the panic in his voice. She took Charlie from Helena's arms and buried her face in the babe's neck, a small, hiccupped sob tearing from her throat. Somehow she knew this would be the last time she held her only child. She breathed in deeply, committing the soft powdery smell to memory. She lifted her head and passed the child back to Helena, her head flicking to the door as the heavy footsteps pounded the ground. Sounds of a scuffle came through the door. Rebecca almost shoved Helena to the cushions, slamming the bench top down above them just as the door swung open.

Charlie squirmed in Helena's arms. She shushed the child softly, trying to hum the song Rebecca had whispered into her daughter's ear. The floor shook under heavy feet. Charlie's frightened cry was drowned by Rebecca's as two gunshots rang through the caravan.

'Sam!' That was Luke's voice, she knew. So they weren't turned off at the thought of killing children.

'Rebecca!' She heard from who she thought may have been James, but the roar of the campervan's engine smothered it quickly.

'Rebecca! No!' It was definitely James who screamed this time.

The van lurched into movement beneath them, picking up speed. Helena heard the voices of the group she had grown so close to fade into the distance.

'Did you really have to shoot them?' The low rasp was right above her as a weight settled onto the seat, cutting off the light.

'We were told to take them all out. She was in the way and we didn't need to keep the hostage. This way we save our bullets. What's the mutt doing?'

Helena frowned. Was there a dog? She heard it then, the scratching at the bench, snuffling at the seat. She held her breath.

'Probably smells the blood on your pants.'

The weight above her leaned back, and the bench groaned. The flippancy grated on her nerves, the only thing holding her still was the heavy presence of the toddler still whimpering on her chest. She pressed her head against her breast to muffle the soft sounds. Helena rested her forehead on Charlie's soft hair and closed her eyes in despair as they left the group behind.

The dog began to growl.

Oh shit oh shit no no no, Rebecca!' James was hysterical, slumped over the lifeless body of his wife where she lay crumpled in the soft dirt. Luke stumbled as he ran, clawing his way to the side of his friend lying prone in the mud.

James's vision darkened at the edges, the world greying into background noise. The oncoming figures that lapped at the fringes of the group, the hysterical crying of his mother behind him. A firm yank at his shirt had him striking out blindly behind him, only distantly registering the yelp of pain as he made contact with someone.

A sharp pain shot through his face and his head jerked to the side. James raised his eyes to meet his father's. His grief reflected back at him. Alex's seemed to be tempered with anger though, lit by a new fire. He grabbed his son's shirt, pulling him up to his feet.

'Those mongrel bikers have your daughter,' he growled. 'And these beasts are standing in the way. We'll come back and bury our dead when we have Charlie back. Get in the truck. Now!'

James spared his beloved one last glance as Alex pulled him laboriously towards the Bushmaster. Slowly, the world beyond his wife's body swam back into focus, his agony reinventing itself as white-hot rage. He jogged determinedly towards the Bushmaster, passing Esther and Anica in his renewed focus. The rear door was open for the group to climb in, and he slid through into the driver's seat, pushing the button to start the engine, drenching the grounds with light as the headlights burned through the dark. He had reached down to release the brake when Alex stopped his hand, panting slightly as though he had run to reach him.

'No, James! We're not all here!' He pointed to the windscreen; Esther and Pete were still outside. They had been backed up to a tree on the far side of the clearing, the space between them and the Bushmaster quickly being eaten up by the infected swarm. Esther was panicking, and Pete was trying desperately to calm her down, even in his own distress. A quick look into the back of the truck showed that the rest of the group had made it in safely.

'Climb, you bastard! Get off the ground!' Luke leaned out of the open roof, gesturing at the tree behind them, begging his brother to get to safety.

Pete scanned the ring of infected that surrounded them, sparing a glance at the truck. He turned and exchanged words with Esther who nodded, and to his surprise, grabbed his face and kissed him determinedly.

Georgia leaned forward between the seats, staring as though she couldn't believe what she was seeing.

Esther looked a little shocked at her own actions but stepped up onto Pete's bent knee, grabbing at the branches above her. Pete shook off his shock and shoved a shoulder underneath her arse, helping her lever herself onto the branch. Once steady, she reached down to grasp his arm.

James could only ascribe the massive lift to the rush of adrenaline that had to be flooding their systems, clearly evidenced by the kiss.

Pete scrambled across to the branch on the other side of the tree just as the clear ground vanished beneath them.

The tableau was lit up with the Bushmaster's yellow light, casting everything in a sickly glow. Pete held a hand up to his eyes to shield them. Even partially hidden, the fear was visible in his face as fingers brushed against the soles of his shoes. He pulled his feet up tightly. Esther had curled up against the trunk as much as she could, face shiny with tears, her knuckles white even from a distance. She looked at the Bushmaster through her hair where it hung limply over her face, her mouth contorting in a silent plea for help.

'What are you waiting for? Go get them!' Luke shoved at the seat in front of him. Alex pulled the young boy back.

James gunned it. The heavy truck shot forward, bumping jerkily over felled bodies that crowded the space in front of them.

'Drive beneath the tree, James.' Alex's voice was calm and steady.

James grabbed desperately to his father's steady nearness to ground him.

Anica hovered behind them, her hand holding onto the handle of the gun turret above her. Alex turned to her as James pulled the Bushmaster to a halt. He stepped forward, leaning into his wife.

'I can do this,' he said softly, resting his hand on hers.

She shook her head. 'No,' she said, placing a hand on his heart. 'You can't.'

James could see his father's face darken, his weaker heart not as strong as his spirit. 'Mum …' he started, standing up.

She smiled at him. 'I'll be fine, I'm just opening the hatch and guiding them in.'

Luke grabbed a gun and made to stand up with her, but she held a hand out to stop him.

'The roof isn't that big. The fewer people we have up there the better.' The shorter woman stepped up onto the seat and pulled the lever. The square hatch pushed upwards with a groan.

Pete and Esther watched carefully as her head and shoulders emerged. Pete pulled his legs up into a precarious crouch, one hand gripping the trunk, the other still clinging tightly to the branch below.

Alex stood below Anica, his brow furrowed in worry as he watched her feet disappearing through the hatch. The clamouring beasts had turned their attention to the noisy truck now amongst them, clawing at the edge of the roof just within reach.

James could follow the hollow sound of her feet where she kept carefully to the centre, avoiding the searching fingers. The tree was directly beside the truck, beneath Pete's huddled form. Anica's steps paused directly above James's head. A thump at the front of the car had every head in the Bushmaster whipping to the front windscreen. Where the bonnet sloped lower, the creatures were able to drape across it, some managing to claw at the window wipers. The thump came from one who had snagged the edge and dragged its body up enough to sprawl across the window, its guttural moan distinctly audible through the glass pane.

'Mum!' Georgia screeched.

'Dad! Get them in, now!' James called back to his father.

Alex had already jumped onto the seat, pushing Luke to the side, his arms grabbing for his wife. James could hear his soft voice demanding that she come back inside, unable to make out her own muffled response.

Movement in the tree showed Pete tentatively swinging down, using the branch as a monkey bar as his feet hit the roof with a thump. Luke looked up as Pete dropped through the hatch to the floor, visibly shaken. He grabbed arms, fingers digging in as he checked his brother over.

'Well at least you got a kiss out of it!' he joked breathlessly, dragging him into a seat. Pete just closed his eyes and let his head sink to his chest.

Anica still stood on the roof. Alex had given up trying to coax her in, and now just stood there, waiting.

A dead housewife had managed to pull herself up onto the bonnet completely, and now turned her attention towards the roof. A man right behind her had stood on something high enough to allow him to crawl after her.

James looked down at the ground as much as the windows allowed, sucking a breath through his teeth when he realised what was happening. In the press of bodies, several of those closest to the truck had been trampled to the ground. Those behind were stepping up onto the piled bodies in a terrifying echo of what he had seen with Sarah at the camping store.

'Dad!' he cried out.

'I can see them!' the frustrated voice bellowed back at him.

James could see Esther had made it to the part of the branch Luke had been sitting on and was hesitating, mouthing something inaudible at Anica.

'Just fucking jump!' James screamed out, thumping a fist against the window. The creatures barely spared him a glance, their attention focused on the women on the roof. James heard his mother slide back suddenly, dancing out of the way of the arms that grabbed at her.

Esther shut her eyes and flung herself off the branch, smacking into Anica and knocking her to the side. Her shaking form blocked the light from the hatch for a moment, her falling body dropping onto Alex and then to the ground.

A scream tore through the air from the roof.

'Mum!'

'Anica!'

The turret hatch slammed down moments before Alex grabbed at the edge, determined to climb out and get to his wife. Her shrill cry broke down into a hacking moan.

James looked on in horror as his mother was dragged down the windscreen. Cruel fingers dug into the skin of her arms, tearing at her throat and hair as they pulled her down to the bonnet, within easy reach of the snarling mass that surrounded them. Greedy fingers and teeth ripped at her clothes wherever they could reach. Blood smeared the glass pane behind her.

Alex threw himself at the back door with a moan that was mournful enough to pass for one of them. Joe and Karen threw themselves at him, leaving Nathan to grab onto Georgia before she tried to follow, pulling her to the ground before she could swing the door open and let the creeping death in to take them all.

'Oh God,' James moaned. His eyes were locked on his mother's jerking form as she slipped from view, and the creatures collapsed in a pile on the ground where she vanished. Joe reached across James's frozen body and switched the headlights off, plunging them into darkness.

Justin felt strangely calm in the thick tension that smothered the truck. Alex was still buried under the pile of people, though he no longer tried to fight them off. The restraining hands had turned into comforting strokes, though from what Justin could see of Alex's face, the preacher was beyond feeling them. James was still frozen in the driver's seat, his quick, shallow pants echoed loudly in the Bushmaster's belly. James shot a look at Seth, who had moved up beside him. The military man jerked his head towards the pile of limbs behind him. Seth grabbed James's shoulders and manhandled his uncooperative legs through the seats to Joe's waiting arms. The archer guided him down to sit on the floor beside his dad.

'What now?' Justin asked, sliding into the driver's seat. The engine still purred softly, almost drowned out by the growls around them.

'Now, we get Charlie and Helena back,' Joe said.

'Why? We don't even know if they're still alive,' Justin muttered under his breath.

Joe glared at him. 'We've lost too many tonight. We need each other to survive this, and if we can get Charlie back, we might get the majority of our group back as well.' He shot a pointed look at the distraught family behind him.

Justin turned back to face the front. 'Fine. Where do we go then? Ballarat's not that small.'

'Let's just get to the city. We can worry about the particulars when we get away from … here.'

Justin shifted the truck into reverse and swung away from the pack of ghouls still huddled over their meal. He turned the wipers on to try to erase the trail of blood that obscured half of the window, only succeeding in smearing it over completely. He dimmed the headlights down to the lowest, relying on his sketchy memory to get them back to the road. The bright red turned a smoky grey in the early dawn.

As they reached the outlying shops that surrounded the gold mining town, the passengers in the back had rallied themselves enough to tune into the quiet conversation in the front, planning how they would get the last two members of their group back safely.

They weaved their way past the crowds of infected staggering through the streets, heading towards the maze of roads that made up the city centre. The larger roads grew more and more congested till Joe directed Justin to pull off into a fast food driveway, parking behind the garishly coloured building to hide the bulky truck.

Joe stood up as tall as he could, pulling everyone's attention to him. 'The roads are too blocked for the truck. The city is still a few blocks from here and we can reasonably assume the rest of the streets are just as bad as what we've seen.'

James narrowed his eyes, almost as though he was expecting Joe to suggest they put the fool's mission to the side and move on.

Joe held up a hand to stall his argument. 'It's still doable, we just need to be smart about this. We need to break into three groups. The first group needs to go through the closer houses around us and get proper clothes.' He gestured towards the clothes they still wore; the few who had come from the city had forgotten about the filthy hospital pyjamas they still wore. 'There are enough houses around here for that, and food and water if you can find it.'

'Let's not waste any more time talking. I need to go get my daughter,' said James.

'And Helena,' Karen added. She and Alex stood to join him.

'Well, we're not getting out the back way. It'll take us right into them.' Nathan said, staring out the small window in the back.

Alex glared up at the turret, the last place he had seen his wife.

'Georgia, Nathan, stay with Seth and the boys, go through the houses. We need a smaller group going into the city. We shouldn't be long, but if we're not back by sunset tomorrow, drive on. Follow the signs to the Grampians.'

Joe pushed the hatch up, and held a hand down to help Karen up to join him. Alex and James climbed up next, looking anywhere to avoid the trail of blood on the roof. They moved to the side, looking over the high fence into the front yard of the next house. Making sure it was clear, Joe jumped onto the green grass, the others following.

Seth called to them softly, drawing their attention back. 'Take these.' He threw the two rifles down to Alex. 'You'll probably need them more than we will, and it's better if we remain silent.' Helena still had the pistol on her when the camper had left, so the rifles were all they had left.

Alex looked up at the roof of the truck, his eyes making contact with his daughter. 'I'll be back soon,' he promised softly before Justin jumped down beside him, taking one of the rifles from his arms.

Georgia looked at the boys beside her in the truck. She could see clearly how shook up they were. A quick glance through the windows reassured her that none of the infected had found them yet, and they were still alone in the driveway.

Try as she might to ignore it, the dark smudge of blood on the front window teased her with its gory tribute. The light had started to spill around them now, the golden veins of the dawn outlining the buildings around them.

'Are you sure you're up for this?' Sam asked, concern bleeding into his voice.

She nodded. 'Save your concern for Pete. Let's do what we need to so we can leave as soon as they get back. *With* Helena and Charlie.'

'Do you really think they'll come back?' Pete hadn't spoken much since they had pulled him into the Bushmaster, still haunted by his brother's death. His face looked flushed, a faint sheen of sweat shining at his temples.

'They have to,' she shot back. She hated that she had to take a leadership position when all she wanted to do was to curl up into a corner and mentally clock out for a week or two.

Nathan rested a hand on her shoulder as Pete and Luke climbed through the roof ahead of them. 'Come on, love, let's see if we can't find you a new pair of shoes.' His soft levity gained no reaction from her, her grief still too thick to appreciate his attempt at comfort.

Seth remained behind with Esther to make sure they had a clear retreat back to safety if they needed it. He picked up the crowbar that James had left behind.

Unbidden, Georgia's eyes fell on the rusty red streaks smeared across the roof. Nathan moved silently to stand in front of her, blocking her line of sight. Her eyes met his and she mustered a weak smile. Gripping her shoulders, he turned her towards the side of the truck where the two young boys waited.

In the time it had taken for Alex to lead the first small group away, two staggering, torn up figures had made their way into the front yard.

Nathan dropped into a crouch, stepping unsteadily out onto the top of the high fence till he stood above one of the infected. Its right arm was little more than the remnants of a shirt that hung in tatters below its shoulder. Its head jerked around to track his movements, its jaw falling open. Nathan swung the crowbar down sharply, the iron splitting skin and meeting bone with a sharp crack that drew the attention of the second. Nathan dropped down to the yard below and stood in a ready stance as the creature fixed on him with milky eyes.

Georgia watched as Nathan stared down the gruesome creature. For the first time she saw it change from a mindless creature to a predator closing in on its prey. She moved to the fence in the same manner Nathan had before her, tracking the figure as it walked in a direct line towards her fiancé.

Nathan lifted the bar to shoulder height, swinging out as the creature stepped within arm's length, collecting it on the side of the head and ripping the ear and a chunk of scalp off its head.

Georgia dropped down quietly to join him. Wasting no time, she snatched up a shovel from where it rested against the fence and drove it down, slicing into the infected man's face and splitting the bridge of its nose. She rested her foot on the flat top of the shovel and drove it down firmly, splitting the skull with the bevelled edge. She jerked the wooden handle, pulling it out with a wet squelch.

A light thump behind her had her wheeling around, bringing the shovel up as she did so. Pete barely managed to duck, the blade slicing through the air where his head had been moments before.

'Sorry,' she whispered, stepping back to make room for Luke to join them. She looked Pete over carefully. 'Perhaps you should stay with Esther? You don't look so good.'

Pete shook his head, resting his forehead against his brother's shoulder. She could see that his face had turned frightfully pale, with the flush of fever highlighted in bright points on his cheeks and brow. Out of habit, Georgia glanced over the boy from head to toe but no wounds or bloodstained clothing hinted at a bite.

Esther had climbed up to the roof, nodding as though to reassure them she would keep watch till they returned. Georgia returned the gesture, turning to look at the double-fronted weatherboard house behind them.

The house could have been ripped straight out of a seventies' sitcom. The carefully manicured lawn led up to a bullnose veranda where a bench swing rocked gently in front of the window. Lace curtains billowed inwards, pushed by the morning breeze through the open window. The only thing that threw the suburban tableau off was the murder of crows that squabbled over an unrecognisable, bloody mess in front of the open door.

A muscle clenched in her jaw, the only visible sign of disgust she allowed herself. As she stepped over the lower step onto the sticky porch, the crows fled in a raucous cloud that had them all ducking as the birds swooped past. Georgia held up a hand to

Nathan, silently asking him to stay behind. She pointed to Luke and gestured him forward.

Nathan turned smartly on his heel, calling Pete to him. He whispered something to the younger man, his words too soft to catch. Pete moved slowly to crouch by the fence closest to the road where he could forewarn them of approaching infected.

Leaving the external work to her fiancé, Georgia tapped Luke's shoulder and gestured to the open door. Taking the lead, she stepped into the darkened hallway, wincing as the door groaned loudly. Georgia led Luke from room to room, wanting to clear the house completely before she let her guard down to look for supplies.

Nothing moved in the old house. All that was left of the family that had once called it home were the clumps of bone and viscera that painted the pale walls and carpet.

The first room made her pause. Luke bumped into her as she froze in place. A canopied crib sat along the far wall, bracketed in by a rocking chair and a tall chest of draws. Georgia felt numb, her traitorous mind replacing the strangers' photos with that of her missing niece. She had been sure she couldn't be surprised by what these inhuman monsters were capable of anymore. The white canopy was stained red and torn in places. She turned to leave the depressing room, pausing as her eyes fell on a tan bear that had fallen to the floor against the wall. Absentmindedly she picked it up, setting it on the rocking chair beside the crib. She could feel its mournful beady eyes on her back as she left the room.

The carpet in the last room was barely visible under the mountains of clothes that lay strewn on every available surface. The dark curtains and propped up guitar marked the room as a teenager's retreat.

'Have a look for clothes in the drawers. They're more likely to be clean. Grab enough for you thr— two, but don't overdo it. I'm going to see what's in the master bedroom for the rest of us.'

Luke nodded and walked to the drawers.

Georgia headed back to the master bedroom, but first paused at the nursery. She grabbed some of the larger clothes that she hoped would fit Charlie. Hesitating, she picked up the lonely bear as well. Perhaps she could give *something* a happy ending, she thought drolly.

She joined Luke at the front door, a small trolley case of clothes at her feet. Luke had thrown what he found in a duffle bag. He had discarded his hospital pyjamas in favour of dark jeans and a button-up shirt. She raised an eyebrow at the neat clothes.

'The good stuff was on the floor,' he explained with a shrug.

A shout and a shot had them running for the front door. Nathan had backed up and was halfway through.

'Pete! Infected!' he panted.

Georgia passed him to help the boy to safety. 'Where is he? Pete! Get in here!'

Nathan pulled her back and shut the door, blocking it with his body when she tried to push him aside.

'No. Pete *is* infected. He's gone.'

Chapter Six
Refuge

Andrew drove in stony silence, his eyes fixed on the road ahead. Guilt, anger and shame gnawed at his stomach in a constant reproach for abandoning the group that had led them safely from Geelong. Tracey fumed beside him in the passenger seat.

He hated that she had been able to talk him into leaving so easily. She had convinced him that their family's safety was in question and they needed to put their son first. He was ashamed he hadn't fought all that hard against the idea.

He glanced into the mirror that had reflected frightened faces behind him till they had been swallowed by shadows.

'Stop it,' Tracey hissed, shooting a glare at him from the corner of her eye. 'Anybody would think you care more for those strangers than you do for your own family.'

Andrew turned his eyes back to the road. He had never been so angry with her in all their years of marriage, but the cold woman he had slept beside for the past month did not resemble the woman he had married in any way.

'It wasn't my family that was abandoned when they needed help the most.' He tried to keep his voice was low and steady. The anger and frustration still bled out despite his attempt to hide it from his son.

They drove wordlessly for hours, stopping only once for Andrew to siphon petrol from a four-wheel-drive that had met a grisly end against a tree. Tracey had kept Mick in the car, standing beside his door with a tyre iron, now their only defence. Andrew ignored the moaning he could still hear inside the crumpled car. If they were still alive, help wasn't coming for them.

Andrew followed the signs to the Grampians; he had been in the house when the group had made contact with whoever had headed out that way. If there was any chance they could find safety in the craggy mountains, he would grab it with both hands. Especially after burning the bridge behind them in such a spectacular fashion.

Andrew's eyes were drooping as he passed the dry fields that surrounded the town, barely registering the lines of abandoned cars that bracketed the road to either side. Tracey dozed in the seat beside him.

'Dad, what's that?' Mick leaned forward between the front seats.

Andrew shook his head, trying clear it from the fog that prevented him from making sense of what lay ahead.

'A train. In the middle of the road.'

He slowed the car till they had stopped in front of the empty passenger carriage that blocked their way, still hooked up to the locomotive, the boom gates standing erect at either side.

'What the hell?' he muttered to himself.

Tracey sat up groggily. 'What's wrong? Do you need me to drive?' Her voice was slurred by sleep as she stretched as much as the cramped quarters allowed.

Andrew rubbed his own neck, feeling the pull of hours of driving that twisted his muscles. 'We're almost there now. Let me get past this and we'll find somewhere to get some rest.' He turned to look over his shoulder, shifting the off-roader into reverse and releasing the break to back up.

He slammed on the brakes, eyes wide. Tracey spun around to see what had spooked him. A white ute, one of the cars that had lined the road, had pulled out and now sat inches away from their bumper. As they watched, two more cars on either side of the road pulled out of the lines and moved to block them, hemming them in completely. He could barely make out the undefined outlines of two people in each car.

'Bugger me, that can't be good,' he cursed under his breath.

Mick darted his head this way and that, trying to watch everything at once. One person from each of the cars stepped out to keep an eye on the road.

'Keep your windows up,' Andrew hissed, unnecessarily, as neither Mick nor Tracey seemed to be reaching to open them any time soon.

Mick shifted into the centre of the back seat to get as far as he could from either side.

A thin, middle-aged man with a mess of red flecked, grey hair walked towards them. He wore a filthy sports coat with what might have once been a white singlet beneath it. A limp bandanna was knotted around his throat. He looked as though he was fighting back an amused chuckle, the lines around his pale grey eyes creased in a hidden smile, striking above his sunken cheekbones. He tapped on the window and gestured for Andrew to roll it down. Andrew didn't bother replying, merely raising his eyebrows and looking pointedly to the front of the car.

An unsmiling young woman with dark hair and sunglasses stood beside the bonnet. She looked at the grey-haired man and levelled a pistol at Tracey's head.

'I won't ask again.' The voice was muted, but clear through the closed window. Andrew pressed the button to lower the window halfway with a soft whirr.

'The name's Blue.' The man spoke softly, leaning back against the last car behind him. He paused as though waiting for Andrew to continue the introductions, sighing deeply when he remained silent. 'Look, mate, this is nothing personal.' He waved a hand to the surrounding cars. 'We gotta be careful who we let in these days, yeah?' He kept his voice calm and matter-of-fact, not offering any hints as to what was going through his head.

Andrew glared at the woman holding his wife at gunpoint. Blue raised a hand towards her and she relaxed, though the gun remained in sight.

'I'm Andrew. We're just looking for a safe place to stay.'

'Well, we do have that. Recently had some vacancies too, so there's enough room to squeeze you and your family in.' He paused. 'If we get that far in the interview of course.'

Tracey grabbed at Andrew's arm; her sudden hope for the safety they offered painfully obvious in her eyes.

Andrew ignored her. 'What interview?' These people could ask for almost anything, and he would most likely give it to them to keep his family safe.

Blue chuckled, the lines around his eyes deepening in amusement. 'Nothing too tragic, mate. We just need to make sure you aren't bringing anything dangerous in with you.'

'You want our weapons? We don't have much.' Andrew was confused. This was a lot of theatre for such a simple request, and reasonable given it was their territory.

'Nah, well yes—for a start. We're more interested in … shall we say … biologically dangerous things.'

'You need to check for bites.' He suddenly understood the need for heightened security.

Blue inclined his head. 'You're going to follow us to the clinic in town. If you check out, Thomas here will drive your car to the camp.'

'Andrew can drive.' Tracey had finally snapped out of her daze, breaking into the conversation with that dogged determination she had worn so much recently.

Blue shook his head, a grin still plastered across his face. 'Andrew will be riding in the back with you and your son.' Blue backed up, walking to the ute and sliding into the passenger seat.

Andrew saw him lift a radio mouthpiece to his mouth. One of the passengers, a solid man a little taller than Andrew, slipped from the car beside them and stood impatiently at his door.

Tracey glared at him. Andrew was too tired to do little more than roll his eyes and open his door, stepping to the ground and around to the rear door. He sighed in relief when Tracey followed him silently.

The train moved slowly forward, making just enough room to allow the strange procession to snake its way down the street at a snail's pace.

The streets were strangely clear once they passed the train tracks. The cars had been moved to the sides of the road, blocking off the side streets completely. Behind the cars were heaped piles of junk. Household items, wooden pallets, garden furniture, everything they could possibly have gotten their hands on had been stacked in such a way that the street beyond was invisible, and, at least by car, inaccessible.

'Dad, what's that?' Mick pointed across him at one of the piles. An orange street cone had been placed carefully in front of a car, a broom sticking out through the top hole. From the top of the broom, just below the brush head, was a green scarf hanging limply at its side.

Andrew shrugged, unable to answer. Each of the barricades they passed boasted the same thing; the only thing that changed was the colour of the improvised flag at the top. This varied between shades of green and red as they moved down the main road. The car ahead jerked to a sudden halt and their silent driver had to slam the brakes on to avoid smacking into the rear. The girl who had pointed a gun at Tracey leapt out of the leading car and jogged past them to Blue's ute. Blue had already lifted the radio mouthpiece and started speaking into it. The girl was gesturing frantically to the barricade they had stopped in front of. The barricade and car were in place like every other street they had passed, but the scarf attached to the pole in front was black. A moment later she was running towards it. With a grace that spoke of practice, she vaulted up the stacked furniture and vanished over the top.

'What's going on?' Tracey asked, bewildered.

'I have no idea.'

Thomas remained silent.

They waited for what felt like an hour, though the clock in the dash suggested it was less than half.

A movement out of the corner of his eye drew Andrew's attention back to the barricade. Towards the top of the pile, a chair shifted slightly. The girl stuck her head over the top before disappearing again. A second later, the curve of her back crested the barricade as she struggled to climb backwards up the accumulated furniture, hauling the limp body of a boy, maybe a few years older than Mick. With them was another boy who alternated between carrying his friend, and a backpack that bounced behind him. Between them, they managed to get the body over the heap and over to the tray of the ute.

Blue stuck his hand out the window and waved his hand sharply. The front car moved forward, setting a quicker pace than they had before. There was a flurry of activity in the ute, where they could see the girl and the new boy fuss over the third, who still lay in the tray out of sight.

The medical centre sat just off the main road, the narrow brown building butting onto a horseshoe-shaped motel. One by one they drove through the tiny gate in front of the motel and into the enclosed car park. The armed girl jumped out of the ute as a man who looked to be in his late thirties ran out of the clinic, the quick response suggesting Blue had radioed ahead. Together, they pulled the injured boy out. From where they sat, it looked like he had started to rouse, his head listing weakly against the jostling as they manhandled him through the doors.

A door to one of the hotel rooms alongside the medical centre opened, and an older woman rushed out to meet them, pushing a wheelchair ahead of her. Together they lifted the semi-conscious boy into it, disappearing back into the room.

Andrew watched the fluid movements of the group, each of them knowing what they needed to do within the ordered chaos. Thomas and the driver of the second car had moved quickly, both now standing to either side of the four-wheel-drive. Blue and the last driver had moved to shut the heavy iron gate behind them and were on their way back.

Blue stopped in front of them, arms crossed casually. Three men joined him to surround the family's vehicle. While not being openly hostile, none showed any signs of welcome for them. Blue beckoned for Andrew to climb down. He hesitated, glancing back to where his son's frightened face stared back at him. Andrew forced himself to smile reassuringly, and stepped down to the ground, hearing Tracey and Mick do the same, shuffling across the seats to stand behind him.

As Tracey stepped within reach, Andrew snagged her hand, pulling her to him. As angry as she could make him, she was his wife, and he would die to protect his family.

Two of the men moved to stand beside Blue, the thin man smiling warmly.

'This is Ivan.' Blue nodded to their driver. The silent man inclined his head. 'Chuck and Damian.' He nodded to the last two. 'They'll take you through to—'

Tracey tensed under Andrew's hand, pulling away and stepping forward, the cowed demeanour replaced by the newly discovered, ill-timed firecracker he was growing used to.

'You'll take us nowhere until we get a proper explanation!' she spat.

'Tracey …' Andrew rested a hand on her arm, begging her to calm down. She shook it off angrily.

'No, Andrew! You just let these people push us around without telling us what they plan to do to us! I just want Mick safe!' Her voice broke a little as her eyes gleamed with a hint of tears. Blinking furiously, she dropped her head to her chest. Andrew stepped up beside her, Mick at her other side. Tracey curled her arms around her son, hiding her head in his hair.

'What on earth are you doing to the poor girl, Blue? The grey-haired woman who had whisked the boy inside stepped out, wiping her damp hands on a towel. A bloody apron covered her brown, sleeveless dress; her red glasses were chipped and sat crookedly on her nose; her sweat-slicked hair was escaping the loose bun atop her head, framing her round face. 'Come inside love, we'll get you a cup of tea and have a good chat.' She walked across to the still sobbing woman, wrapping a bare arm around her shoulders and steering her unresisting form into the room. She shot a sharp look at Blue, who rolled his eyes and stepped aside to let them pass. Andrew and Mick followed them through.

'You know we have to follow protocol, Gwen. It's the only thing that keeps us safe.'

She tutted harshly over her shoulder as she steered Tracey through a hole that had been broken through the back wall of the motel room, permitting them access to the uncomfortably warm clinic beyond.

'Tameka, let the poor boy rest,' she called down the hall. 'Christopher is doing everything he can and your hovering won't help. Put the kettle on dear.' Gwen ignored Andrew completely, pushing the distraught Tracey into a chair.

The young girl who had held the gun on Tracey poked her head out of a door down the hall.

'It's Tam,' she said with the surliness of a teenager who's had the same unsuccessful argument several times in the past. Gwen shot her a sharp look. 'Kettle.'

'Yes, ma'am.' She flicked off an insolent salute and moved across the hall to a tiny kitchenette.

The man who had helped bring the wounded boy from the car poked his head out of the room and crooked a finger towards them. Andrew looked at him, confused, until Damien peeled away from the group, walking into the room he had zipped back into.

'How do you still have power here?' Andrew asked.

Blue threw himself into a chair across from him. 'A power station keeps working unless the lines are completely down. We haven't had any major accidents around here, so we're good.'

Andrew's surprise must have shown on his face because Blue went on. 'I worked as a sparky before all of this. It's how we managed to get power up to the campsite as well, but you'll probably see all that later.'

The girl came back with a stained tray, crowned with a ring of gently steaming cups.

'Thank you, Tameka.' Gwen stood and took the tray from her, placing it on the exam table to the side of the room. She handed out the cups as Tam rolled her eyes and wordlessly returned to the room Damien had vanished into.

Gwen pressed a warm cup of black tea into Tracey's hand. 'Don't mind her, she's very close to Caleb. Those kids go back way before all this. They'll be worried about the quarantine.' Her own worried eyes flicked to the closed door.

'Quarantine?' Tracey asked, her voice still a little tremulous.

'It's part of the protocol. If you're injured on a run you spend a week in quarantine, up at J Ward. Just as a precaution.' Her voice was steady with the practiced calm of someone used to dealing with hysterical patients and agitated family members.

'And if they get sick?' Tracey's hands tightened around the cup in her hands. It sloshed slightly as she brought it up to her mouth.

Gwen either didn't hear, or chose to ignore the question, standing to wash her hands. 'Okay, dear, I need you to ask your son and husband to step out of the room for us now. If you don't want him to see you in the altogether, that is.' She kept her words soft with a gentle smile, intended to relax her.

It failed.

'Excuse me?' Andrew could see Tracey's hackles starting to rise again.

Gwen held up a hand, but stood her ground. 'I understand that it's an intimidating prospect, but I'm sure you understand we cannot allow anyone who may have been exposed to the infection to take it to the camp. We can't afford to allow anybody up there who will put our families at risk.'

Blue had been content to allow Gwen to carry the conversation till this point. Andrew got the impression this was usual behaviour, allowing Gwen's calm demeanour to relax any newcomers. He leaned forward in his chair now; his natural leadership making him take control of the conversation once more.

'This is for your protection as well. If you and your family are cleared to join us, I'm sure you would insist on any newcomers undergoing the same precautions.'

Gwen moved to the door and held it open. 'I can assure you, you are in professional hands. I am a qualified nurse. Your son and husband can stay together just outside the door while we get this done, and they'll be within shouting distance the whole time.'

Tracey looked unconvinced but nodded at Andrew and Mick. They stepped outside where Blue was waiting for them.

'She won't be long. In the meantime, I'll do my best to answer any questions you might have so far.'

'Where to start?' Andrew asked, only half joking.

'Let me start then.' Blue leaned casually against the wall behind them. 'When all this started, most of the towns around here headed for the hills. There was a rumour that the dingo fence was being reinforced and guarded, but many decided the risk wasn't worth the trip. Then there were the rumours of people not being heard from after they left if they did head up there. We had hundreds of terrified people, all scurrying through the hills. We didn't have our protocols in place at that time.'

His eyes were distant, fixed on an aerial photo of the town that hung in the clinic's hallway, the imposing crest of the Grampians in the distance. 'My family and I were lucky, we got pulled into a group who knew the mountains well, and about forty of us made it to Boronia Peak. We blocked off the path completely, cutting off all access on the city side. What we didn't realise was that some of the people in the group had brought the infection with them. It hadn't been obvious though—they didn't have any of the signs we've come to expect. They managed to turn some of the camp in their first night, and with our only path out of the peak blocked off, we were easy pickings. Fifteen people died that night, my wife included. Another twenty took off the next morning, took a good chunk of what we had brought up with us.' He laughed humourlessly. 'We lost over half our group before we even set up camp.' He looked at Andrew, not turning his head as he did so. 'Now we make sure no one brings the infection into camp.'

'How do you do that if some of them show no signs?' Andrew asked.

'Trade secret,' Blue said with a smile. 'Let's just say the whisperings we pick up can be quite helpful sometimes.'

Ivan walked back to them, handing a beer to Blue, Andrew and Chuck, keeping one for himself. Andrew took it with a furrowed brow.

'On the way here, along the street, why bother barricading it at all? Why not avoid the city altogether?' Andrew twisted off the top and sipped, savouring the bitter brew.

'We're cautious, not heartless. We know people will be coming through if they survive the mess in the cities, and they're welcome to join whichever group has room. Still, every person has to be checked out. Each town around the Grampians is set up in a similar manner and other roads that might bypass the towns are blocked off. One person manages the watchers posted in each town, sending smaller groups down to assess the threat. That's what we were doing when we met you. Newcomers are taken to the designated clinic and checked over. It's our first line of defence.'

'And if they've been bitten?' Mike piped up.

'Each town has a quarantine outside of city limits. Ours is J Ward.'

Mick looked suddenly intrigued. 'Isn't that the prison for the criminally insane?'

'Years ago, yes. It has rooms for isolation, working kitchens and bathrooms. Everyone there gets the best care, including the carers staffed there at all times.'

'Plus, the grounds have a great veggie garden and hobby farm for the camp.' Ivan grinned proudly.

'Ivan here was a farmer. He's invaluable to the group. At his hands we've enough fresh food to feed our camp, and trade with the others.' Their silent driver smiled for the first time, revealing crooked teeth with faint tobacco stains.

'Why not just make that the first station then?' Andrew frowned, frustrated at the lengthy detour the conversation had taken.

'Because you can't trust everyone.' Blue's face darkened momentarily. 'Plus, this is already outfitted for modern medical care, and the hotel at the back means this place is completely secured with rooms available if we need them. J Ward is for *after* the immediate health concerns have been attended to. If they haven't turned within the week, we blindfold the newbies and take them to camp.'

'And if they turn?' Andrew had noticed that all three times the question had been asked, Blue had skirted the answer. He was sure he knew the answer but had to ask anyway.

Blue just raised an eyebrow, still not answering, letting him fill in the blanks on his own.

'And the boy you brought in?'

'Will be taken to J Ward as soon as the doctor and Tam patch him up.'

Mick opened his mouth, frowned, and closed it again, shaking his head.

'Go on, ask your question,' Blue prompted.

'What were the flag things in front of the barricades?'

Blue looked as though he would keep silent for a moment before deciding otherwise. 'We try to only take what we need so we don't take up unnecessary room up at camp and supplies are left if other groups need them. Green means there are still shops on the street that can be checked for supplies, red means it's been tapped out.'

'And the black?' Andrew asked, thinking back to the young man who had been hauled over the makeshift wall.

'Help,' Chuck muttered simply, absentmindedly rubbing at a barely visible scar on his arm.

They looked up as Tameka walked out of the room down the hall, wiping clean, wet hands on her jeans.

'He's unconscious,' she stated. 'There's a large tear in his thigh. It cut into the muscle, close to the artery. Doc got it sewn up pretty tightly. Says if he doesn't turn, it'll be a while before he's walking again.' She sounded tired. 'We'll move him as soon as they finish with the restraints.'

'Restraints?' Mick sounded startled, his head whipping around to look at the door she had closed behind her.

'It's standard procedure. If he's infected, we don't want him loose in the car when it takes over,' Blue explained casually.

A fit young man poked a stubbled face out the door, scratching his neck tiredly.

'Ivan, Damien's got him secured. Can I have you in here for transport please?' Ivan grunted and walked over.

'Just the one for transport, Doc?' Chuck asked, glancing up.

Ivan paused and looked back at Blue, his eyes shifting not so subtly towards Andrew and Mick. Blue jerked his head in a 'go on' motion.

'We'll be right. Ivan and Damien will stay here. They can organise additional transport if needed,' he reassured them. 'Doc, are you right to do an admission check now?' Blue asked as the door they were standing in front of opened, releasing a flushed Tracey into the hallway. She moved to stand beside her husband, fastening the last button of her shirt as she did so, then pulling her sleeve down to cover the cotton wool taped to her inner arm.

'That took a little longer than I thought it would,' Andrew queried, eyeing her from head to feet, reassuring himself that all was well. She reached out and clasped his hand.

The young doctor approached them with a tired smile, nodding to Ivan as he moved past him into the room. 'Will you be coming in together or would you prefer one on one?' he asked. 'It is quite a thorough exam so consider carefully how much you want each other to see.'

Tracey flushed deeper, dropping her head against Andrew's shirt to avoid eye contact.

'I'll go first,' Andrew volunteered, stepping forward. He followed the doctor, pressing himself against the wall as Damien and Chuck pushed a wheelchair out of the room.

Caleb's slumped form looked small, his arms bandaged together from shoulder to shoulder, hands cradled in front of him. The bandages looped around the arms of the chair, holding him fast where he sat, his legs similarly constrained. The injured leg rested on a plank of wood that sat under his rump, keeping it straight.

'Will he be all right?' Tracey sounded concerned, watching as they wheeled him carefully out of the room that broke through to the motel.

'Time will tell,' the doctor murmured, promising nothing. He held out a hand to Andrew with a wry smile. 'I'm Raigan, and I'll be conducting your strip search today.'

Chapter Seven

Reunions

Matt drove with an intense focus. Even with the carnage vanishing behind them, he could not convince the muscles in his legs to unclench as he bore down on the accelerator. His eyes were fixed on the road ahead, his only movement the stiff shift of his arms as he changed the course of the heavy vehicle to avoid the larger obstacles. As he cleared a sharp bend, scattered pieces of a mover's truck had him jerking the wheel to avoid the wreckage.

'Watch it!' Sarah barked. He winced but remained silent. 'Ahh, shit, Meghan. Don't you dare,' Sarah muttered.

He spared a quick glance into the rear-view mirror. Sarah stooped over Meghan's still, pale form stretched over the seats.

She had been like that since they had raced from Geelong. Sarah pressed her hands hard into Meghan's stomach, pulling a moan from the barely conscious prone girl's.

'Is she okay?' Josh's worried face hovered over Sarah's shoulder. His attention hadn't wavered from them as she worked frantically to close the gaping hole in Meghan's stomach. Jim had grabbed a first-aid kit from their collection, tearing it apart and looking to Sarah for direction.

'I need something to suture the wound together,' Sarah panted, rubbing her forehead on her arm.

Josh looked around blankly, the first-aid contents spilling over the floor of the truck. 'I can't … there's nothing …'

Matt could hear the stress tearing at his voice.

'There's nothing but fucking bandages and tape!' He threw the bag onto the floor, running his fingers through his hair. He paused, caught by something at his feet. He ducked down, jumping back up to proffer what looked to be a small sewing kit from the pile. 'What about this?'

'It'll do!' Sarah rubbed her face on her shoulder. 'Grab the mattress needle—no, the curved one, that one, yes. Now thread it. Quickly!'

'I've never done this before!' he moaned.

Matt could only imagine what was going on, sports-mad Josh trying to thread a tiny needle with clumsy fingers. The tension coupled with the ridiculous image it presented had him choking out a hysterical giggle. He glanced back to the road, the black ribbon unspooling itself beneath them as they sped from the city.

'Oh, I'm sorry.' Sarah's voice seemed to pick up a waspish quality. 'Would you like to swap jobs?'

Even from the front seat Matt could see Josh's face turn slightly green at the thought.

'Use the bloody threader!' she was yelling now.

Josh startled and glared at her.

Sarah closed her eyes for a moment, sucking in a deep breath. 'Please! I don't have a spare pair of hands.' She turned her head to face him. 'I need your help.'

'I'm sorry,' he muttered, pulling out the oddly shaped metal piece and following Sarah's explanation to pull the cotton through the needle before pressing it into her sticky red fingers.

Jim had reluctantly moved behind the driver's seat to give

them room to work. Josh grabbed his arm from behind him, pulling Matt's attention back to the road in time to swerve around an unidentifiable mass in the centre of the road.

Matt heard Sarah curse behind him as he brought the car under control. 'Sorry! Sorry!' he called back, flicking his eyes up to the mirror to check they were okay. Jim seemed to have completely disappeared from view.

Matt hazarded a glance over his shoulder. Josh was leaning against his seat, bloodstained hands clasped tightly around his chest. Meghan's soft moans punctuated the tension that threatened to suffocate them as the pain kept her semi-conscious under Sarah's hands.

What felt like hours later, Sarah slumped back onto the seat. Her hands were coated in shiny red that might have given the impression of satin gloves if not for the occasional dribble from fingers that hung limply between her knees, falling in hypnotic drips to the floor. Her eyes were closed, and she looked pale and drained, like she had shrunk within the last few hours.

'What happened, Joshua?' Jim's voice was steady. He passed over a wet rag to Sarah, who roused enough to rest it against her face before she seemed to lose the momentum and left it there. The excess water carved trails in the grime that covered her face.

'I'm not ... We were careful,' Josh stuttered uncertainly. 'We moved slowly, kept to the centre aisles, and only grabbed what we needed. Meghan had already started piling what she could into the bags at the front.' He glanced at the bulging shopping bags on the floor. Most were still intact. One lay tipped over the floor haemorrhaging first-aid kits. 'Some of the stuff we needed was at the back. We could see it! It was right there. We thought we'd make it quick, keep quiet. There wasn't any movement, no noises, nothing. We had heard a bang before but it was distant, like it wasn't in the store.'

Jim winced. 'That was us.'

'Well it didn't seem to trigger anything where we were. We figured if nothing had come from that, we could split up. Not far!' he hurried on as Sarah looked up sharply. 'I went to get the camping gear, she was one aisle over getting the rest, for cooking and shit.' He stood up and moved to Meghan, combing his fingers through her sticky hair. 'We got careless. We moved most of the bags to the truck. I was on the way back to the store. She was still in there, packing the last one when I heard her scream. I ran to where I left her. Her head was yanked right back. One of the bastards had reached through the shelves and was pulling her hair.' His face contorted into a scowl and he scrubbed a hand across his eyes. 'There was no noise. It had something tight around its throat stopping it from making noise.'

'Like a collar?' Sarah asked hesitantly. She had almost forgotten about the collared creatures, so fixated on escaping that she had allowed the peculiarity to fall from her memory. Now here they were again.

Josh frowned and shook his head. 'No, like rope. For tents. I froze. I couldn't think straight. I know I fell against the wall, must have pushed something because that screech … I think I set an alarm off. It was enough to distract the thing so that Meghan could pull free but she fell onto the next shelf. Something fell on top of her and I snatched it off her … *out* of her.' His eyes skittered to a bloody axe that had been flung under the seats. 'God. I'm so sorry, Meghan.'

The adrenaline that had kept him talking almost visibly drained from him and he slumped on the seat at Meghan's head, lifting it to rest on his lap. Sarah picked up her wrist, feeling for a pulse.

'Will she be okay?' Josh asked softly.

'Honestly? I don't know,' she replied, placing Meghan's hand back on her chest. 'She lost a lot of blood and I have no way to get more into her. No to mention the risk of infection or the possibility I've missed something.' She rested her head in her hand. 'I've never done this before.'

Jim sat beside her, resting an arm across her slumped shoulders.

Matt slowed the truck to a crawl and pulled over to the side of the road, turning in his seat to face them. 'Um, you might want to see this.' He moved aside to reveal the windscreen. The afternoon sun glared through the window.

Hedging the road ahead was the most macabre collection of scarecrows lining either side, bloated and discoloured. Some were missing limbs, or in spectacular case, the entire lower half of its body.

'… the hell?' Sarah breathed. The creatures still moved, pinned in place by a stake driven through them and into the ground like the world's ugliest butterfly collection.

Green, mottled arms reached towards the stationary vehicle, the stakes tearing at their flesh, leaving gaping wounds where they protruded through necks or between ribs. Teeth marks and exposed bone on their legs hinted at scavengers that had taken advantage of the restrained meat.

'I think I'm going to be sick,' Sarah groaned.

Jim let out a low whistle. 'What kind of twisted mongrel would do this?'

'Let's not hang around to find out.' Josh hadn't moved from where he sat with Meghan's head on his lap, but even his low vantage point was not enough to block the morbid view.

Matt looked out at the broken down shell of a store that still boasted signs of a skirmish. Clear bike tracks had left churned up clumps of dirt in the front parking lot. He eyed the dark building warily as he pressed down on the accelerator and moved past the mockery of an honour guard.

Sarah kept her head down until they were well out of sight, focusing on Meghan instead. Although her attention was fixated on the girl, the low moan that escaped her lips still caught her off guard.

'Meghan? Are you okay? Can you hear me?' Sarah picked up a pale wrist, fingers feeling for the pulse. 'Shhh, stay still, that's it.' Sarah kept her voice low. 'Her pulse is still weak, but if she's waking up, she can drink something to try to get her blood pressure up.'

'Sweetheart?' Josh still sounded worried, not daring to move. 'Can you open your eyes for me?'

Matt couldn't see her face, but from the grin that split Josh's face he was sure she had done just that.

Josh poured a little water on a torn scrap of fabric, wiping it over her mouth softly. The cool water must have woken her as she almost jerked upright, only Sarah's hands keeping her down. Greedy hands came up to grab at the wet cloth and she held it to her face, sucking desperately at the moisture held there, and pushing it away in disgust when it ran dry. Sarah grinned, tipping a little more onto the cloth for Josh to repeat the action, gradually managing to tip half of the bottle down her parched throat.

Matt pulled over to the side of the road, twisting in his seat to face them.

'We're just outside Ballarat now. I think they might not be accepting tourists anymore though.' He gestured to the side where a small shop sat ready to greet incoming travellers. The ground was churned up and marred by a mess of tyre tracks, with several corpses half covered by the disturbed mud.

Sarah let out a low whistle as she saw the carnage. 'It seems that Geelong isn't the only one with a biker problem.' She pointed out the snaking patterns of single tyres that weaved their way back onto the road and into the city. Matt felt her freeze, her still out-stretched finger wilting a little as she stared at the muddy corpses.

'Bec?' she whimpered. Catching Matt off guard, she threw herself across his lap, managing to push the door open before he caught on and grabbed hold of her waist, holding her back from tumbling outside. 'No! Let me go!' she yelled, eyes locked on the tangled blond hair she clearly recognised. 'Please! Bec!' Sarah was sobbing now, pushing at Matt's restraining hands.

'Okay, we'll go together, but you need to calm down first. You'll bring all the fuckers that did this right back if you don't.' He let the hint of a plea soften his voice, hoping to appeal to her rational side. He shot a look over at the others. Josh stayed seated on the backseat, Meghan's head in his lap. Even through the painful grimace, Meghan had pity etched into her face as she watched her friend fall to pieces in front of her. Jim moved behind Sarah, pulling her back enough to allow Matt to open the door and slide out from under her shaking form. Matt turned back to help her down, taking most of her weight as she seemed to slump against him. They picked their way across the soft ground, her tremor growing worse as they drew close enough to see her lifeless face, half-covered by pale blond hair. Sarah turned white, sinking to her knees beside her to brush the hair aside. Her hand fluttered weakly towards a smaller body flung to the side, a bullet wound clearly visible in his forehead. Matt thought he heard a whispered 'Sam' leave her mouth, but she made no move to stand.

Until she saw the last body.

Lifting her head from her sister's body, her face melted, falling into silent agony before she clambered to her feet, clutching at Matt's arm for support. Throwing herself forward on unsteady feet, she stumbled towards a tree close by. Matt hurried to keep up, reaching her in time to see her pull a bloody scarf to her cheek. He snatched it from her, quickly wiping furiously at the red smear it left on her skin.

Sarah looked up at him, her eyes appeared lifeless at the sight of the corpses that littered the ground around them. 'Mum,' she sobbed. 'They got my mum.'

Jim cradled Sarah against him on the bench, stroking her hair gently. The truck had been silent since Matt had helped Jim drag her near unresponsive form back onto the backseat.

They slipped over the roads into the strangely still city. Too soon, trees gave way to houses and shops, clumping together to form the dense suburbs that skirted the city. Sarah lifted her head to glance through the small window before sitting up completely. Jim frowned as he almost felt the physical shutdown as she pulled a blank mask over her face. He could see Meghan checking her over as well, no doubt looking for the same cracks that he himself was watching for.

Sarah ignored them, turning her attention to the front. 'Matt, is there somewhere we can stop for a while? I need a little fresh air.'

Matt snorted inelegantly. 'Air I can do. *Fresh* might be pushing it.'

Through the window between the two front seats, Jim could see the staggering figures of ex-residents milling about the streets. Some had started to show advanced signs of decay, their bloated, mottled bodies and tattered clothing attracting flies and insects in droves.

'What are the odds of finding anywhere safe to stop?' Matt huffed.

'What about in there?' Jim asked, pointing to the drive-through that snaked behind a fast food outlet. In the face of so few alternatives, Jim suggestion went undebated.

Matt steered the heavy truck in the indicated direction. 'Woah. What ...'

Five pairs of eyes looked up to see what looked like the back of their own truck. The only difference between the truck in front of them and the one they currently called home was the spray of bullet holes pockmarked in the rear panel.

A rounded face peeked down at them from the roof, twisting in surprise before it zipped back out of sight. Sarah jerked at his side.

'Can we back up?' Jim offered.

Sarah wrenched herself from her seat with a shaky 'No', and for the second time threw herself at the door, this time successfully flinging it open. Barely glancing at the road, she stumbled out onto the concrete. Jim followed close behind, pushing the door shut behind him.

'Esther? Esther, is that you?' Sarah softly called out to the top of the truck.

Jim saw the round face reappear, followed by a heavy body as a pair of legs swung around to find purchase against the door before slithering down to the ground.

'Sarah?' The girl looked to be in shock. 'But you're dead.' She approached them slowly, her eyes locked on Sarah's face.

Jim glanced around them nervously. Their presence had not gone unnoticed by the things in the street. They had now started converging on their trucks.

Sarah stepped in close to the girl, resting her hands on her shoulders and breathing a sigh of relief. Stepping back slightly, she glanced at the truck behind them.

'Is James here? Dad? Are they okay?'

Jim stepped closer to them. 'Girls, I'm sorry to interrupt, but we really need to move this somewhere safer.'

Sarah glanced back at him, eyes widening as she finally caught sight of the audience they had attracted. Esther pulled the door open behind her, waving back the tall shadow that appeared in the doorway. Sarah raised a hand that was enveloped by a larger, male hand from within, pulling her into the shadows, Esther raising her hand for the same service.

Jim barely hesitated before climbing in after them. He squinted into the darkness, the shadows slowly shifting to reveal Sarah standing beside the stranger, Esther on her other side. His jaw tightened instinctively, fists clenching slightly as he fought the sudden urge to pull her to his side and away from the unknown man. He was broken out of his distraction by the man's rough voice.

'... know Esther, I'm Seth.' He extended his hand for Sarah to shake; the gentility looked odd in the circumstance.

A thump on the roof had them all looking up in time to see the hatch above them open, blinding them with the sudden spill of sunlight.

'Seth? What's with the twin truck?' The light voice that drifted down through the hatch next had Sarah's full attention, a sob catching slightly in her throat as a second woman dropped through, stilling as she caught sight of the newcomers.

'Sarah?' Jim stepped towards her, concerned.

'Georgia?'

At Sarah's hoarse call, another silhouette eclipsed the hatch. 'Sarah? It … you … Oh my God, you're all right!'

The two women stood barely inches from each other. Jim could see the similarities in their eyes that marked her for the sister Sarah had spoken of. Neither seemed able to make the first move.

Seth not so subtly stepped forward and elbowed Sarah's sister in the back, sending her tripping into Sarah's arms, which closed around her tightly.

A sudden dark had them blinking rapidly as the hatch above them shut behind another person. Another man stepped forward and embraced both of the sisters where they hadn't released each other. Sarah had started sobbing softly again, her shaking shoulders betraying her confused emotions.

Jim thought he heard her whimper 'Mum' among the jumble of choked out words that vanished into her sister's shirt. Seth grimaced and glanced at the windscreen where smears of red still webbed the glass at the sides.

A flash of light pulled their collective attention to the rear window, the second truck flashing their high beams a second time to flood the truck with light.

'We should tell them what's going on.' Sarah's voice was choked, and she wiped a hand firmly across her face as she straightened reluctantly.

Jim stepped forward, placing himself between Sarah and Seth. 'Let's just call them on the radio. We know what station they'll be on.' He pushed his way to the front and slipped into the passenger seat before picking up the receiver and dialling into the frequency they had been using.

'Hello?' Meghan sounded stressed, her sharp voice snapping through the speakers. 'Sarah? Jim?'

Sarah frowned. 'What's she doing up?' she muttered. 'She's supposed to be resting.'

'We're fine,' Matt reassured her. 'Sarah says you're supposed to be resting.'

'Yeah? Tell her I would be if someone hadn't climbed into a stranger's car!'

'We, uh …' He glanced back at the group. 'We bumped into old friends.'

'The two that hopped over the fence?' Matt laughed. 'I had to stop Meghan from running out after you when they piled in. Your dash seemed to attract a bit of attention—you'll find it harder to get back,' he warned.

'We'll find out what's happening here and then figure something out,' Jim said.

'Okay, just give us a signal if you need a rescue!' Meghan's pained voice didn't support the vague threat, and Seth chuffed out a laugh, earning a glare from Jim.

'We will,' Jim promised.

Sarah moved to the tiny window at the back, flashing thumbs up to the truck behind them and laughing weakly at whatever they did in response.

Jim put the receiver back in its place and stood beside Sarah, still making sure to place himself between her and the imposing man, who had not taken his eyes from her. Her sister stepped up close and pulled Jim into a firm hug. Frantically he looked to the other men for a rescue, but each of them avoided his eyes, except Seth who shot him a smirk.

'Thank you,' she whispered into his neck. 'Thank you for bringing my sister back to me.'

Chapter Eight

The Monster

Dr Marcus hunched over his microscope, the evening sunlight shrouding the room in shadows. The mask he now wore gave him an odd, bulbous appearance. Peta watched him in silent revulsion from her cage. On the steel table behind him lay his latest victim, tied securely. Long blond hair draped over the edge of the table where the scalp was peeled back to expose the skull and brain to the rooms' occupants.

It wasn't dead yet.

Arching against the restraints that held it secure, it emitted a wet, rasping growl, filling the otherwise silent room.

The madman had left the brain in place for now, subjecting it to a range of treatments. The room still stank from where he had wired his previous subject to a generator, reducing the infected man to a silent, writhing mass of nerves arcing off the table under the current. He had repeated the test at intervals till the smoking corpse had completely stopped responding to the continued brutalisation.

Dr Marcus was growing increasingly distracted, muttering to himself as he worked into the evening. Peta watched silently, her throat dry and achy from the lack of food and water. Her tears had dried up halfway through day two.

Absorbed as he was in his work, the obsessed doctor seemed to have pushed all thoughts of her to the side, consigning her to little more than a passing distraction.

Heaped up in the far cage, several corpses sprawled over each other. Infected blood mixed with non-infected as it seeped into the carpet in an indistinguishable sticky red mess.

They lay there, like her, discarded once his use for them had passed, making room on the table for the next. She barely noticed the stench of rot anymore, having grown used to the stomach-churning odour.

Peta was starving. She hadn't eaten since she had been taken, and to her disgust, her eyes had lingered on the bloody meat on the floor beside her more than once.

In the cage immediately beside her, an obese man lay slumped on the floor. He hadn't woken up since he had been unceremoniously dumped there. His arm had been methodically sliced, one long thin line running from elbow to wrist. The doctor had smeared infected saliva on the wounds before injecting him with a translucent yellow liquid in a test similar to what she surmised had been performed on her without the invasion of a tissue graft. Her bandages were off now; she had removed them herself after realising he had no interest in her wellbeing. She had two long parallel scars running from wrist to elbow, the edges red, but fortunately not infected as far as she could tell. A patch of skin three shades darker than her own stood out against her own pale skin halfway down her arm.

There had been a girl before him who had screamed for a full day, ripping at her skin as she reacted violently to whatever she was given before the doctor had slit her throat in an uncharacteristic display of mercy, though he could easily just have had enough of the noise. The fat man's angry red skin around the site of the incision had swollen to the point where it resembled a split sausage on a grill, bleeding freely. Sweat beaded on his pasty brow and he murmured fitfully in his pained sleep.

The doctor glanced over at him and frowned, turning back to his microscope and scribbling in the notebook. Her co-prisoner's breathing stuttered, his pained but steady rasps changed into choppy, reedy gasps, spraying droplets of blood down the front of his soiled shirt. They slowed down till at times she wasn't sure he was breathing at all. She watched, unable to tear her eyes away as he breathed his last. A viscous strand of bloody drool spilt from his open mouth as his head fell forward against his chest.

'Damn it!' Dr Marcus swore, slamming a hand on the desk in front of him. Pushing his chair back violently, he stalked over to the cages, pushing the mask onto his forehead. The now deceased man sat in a growing pool of blood as it crept across the floor of the cage and into Peta's, the sticky border rolling over itself in its attempt to escape.

Peta backed up as far as she could, her back pressed hard against the solid bars, unable to do anything but grimace as the blood reached her curled form, soaking into her clothes like a sponge. She whipped her hand up to cradle it against her chest as the still warm fluid teased at her fingers.

Her eyes fixated on the red drips that left trails down her skin. As though in a trance, she brought her sticky fingers before her eyes, the red liquid mocking her thirst. Her parched tongue stuck to the roof of her mouth. She brought her finger to her lips, closing her eyes as the thick fluid touched her tongue, the first hint of moisture she had tasted in days. She dipped her finger in again, bringing it to her mouth eagerly before pressing her entire hand into the puddle, cleaning it off with enthusiastic kitten licks, dipping it in and licking it clean each time she had removed the last trace from her skin.

Lost in the pleasure of having something that soothed her ravenous hunger, she didn't notice as she scooted closer to the other side of the narrow cage. Her fingers reached through the bars to clench the bloody shirt tightly, pulling the cooling body tightly against the bars that separated them and licking the blood that fell to his chin.

Dr Marcus stood still, eyebrows rising in sudden interest as he took in the new development. Patient 61 had pulled the body in the next cage towards her and had buried her face in his neck, her fingers dug into the exposed flesh of his forearm, fingers tearing bloody gouges as she lost herself to a new and baser nature. Intrigued, the doctor stood up, approaching the cages slowly so as not to distract his living specimen. It had been the only one to survive for so long.

His control subject.

He had spoken with his contacts several times concerning her. He knew her resilience related to an existing mental illness, and his own studies had been backed up by his partners' limited observations. He had decided to allow her to deteriorate without input and assess how the virus affected the expiration period of this new mutation. Now, though, he would need to keep her around. He had to see what the next stage in this de-evolution was.

Dr Marcus heard the distinctive snap of bone as she pulled the arm against the bars in an attempt to bring it closer to her mouth. In her desperate frustration, she had yanked it through, bending it at an unnatural angle to force it to fit and snapping one of the thinner bones in the forearm. She gripped the larger portion of the arm firmly; pulling at it where it barely clung to the body. Blunt teeth sunk into the limb, the forced starvation having no doubt left her desperate for sustenance.

He crouched by the cage, entranced at the new aspect of the disease that had revealed itself. His movement drew her eyes up to him, though she continued to chew the flesh and muscle, clutching it close as if afraid he would deny her this too. Her eyes were free of the unfocused film that seemed characteristic of the infection he had observed so far. He frowned at the sharp clarity that peered back at him, no signs of self-disgust or shame on her face, only a curiosity that mirrored his own. She cocked her head as he made to stand up. With a vicious lunge, she buried the jagged piece of bone that still protruded from the arm into his chest.

The doctor looked down in pained shock as the arm seemed to twitch in time with his own thumping heartbeat. His hands fluttered up weakly to grasp at the cold hand that protruded from his ribs before falling limply to his knees.

Peta watched dispassionately as her captor bled out on the floor. At the first taste of blood, her inhibitions had vanished, no longer registering it as a human who had been breathing only moments before; she was only driven with the need to replicate, to spread the virus. With the sharp edge of her hunger dulled a little, her rational mind seemed to take over once more.

As the doctor fell to the floor with a wet gurgle, she reached out between the bars, pulling at his clothes and pawing at the pockets till she was rewarded with the sharp jangle of keys. Her hand shook slightly as she inserted the key and turned it, standing up as the door fell open to her touch and rested against the doctor's still form. She gave it a vicious kick, pushing him aside violently. She stepped out, stretching to her limit for the first time in what must have been near a week.

She stooped over his body, the shallow wet wheeze signalling that the doctor yet lived. Her bloody fingers gripped his chin, turning him to face her. Lowering her head till her hair brushed his cheek, she kissed him, her teeth grabbing and tearing at his lip till it was torn from his face.

Peta walked over to the window, squinting as the evening sun brushed over her face. Now that the churning hunger had released her from its claws, exhaustion started to pull at her bones.

The window looked out onto the unknown buildings of the university, recognisable only by the large sign that adorned the grey concrete of the building across from her. Her scavenging group had walked far enough to know that one of the still open entrances to the tunnels had to be nearby.

Behind her, the doctor twitched.

Peta rummaged through the cluttered desk and turned up half a bottle of water and five red notebooks, similar to the one that lay closed on the top of the desk. All were filled with the doctor's cramped, barely legible writing from cover to cover. The macabre collection of brains and carefully boxed slides took up the majority of the desk space, spilling out to fill boxes on the floor. Peta swept an arm across the top of the desk, sending the samples to the floor in a wet mess. Tissue and chemicals splashed up the side of the wall, slipping down and leaving trails in their wake, like sauce-covered pickle slices thrown at restaurant walls. Hesitating a moment, Peta grabbed the notebooks, cradling them in her arms before walking briskly into the corridor.

Milky eyes in a torn face flickered open as the doctor stirred once more.

The genetics building that had been turned into the doctor's playground led out onto a small service street, the crowded buildings offering no clue as to which of the still quiet paths she should take. Peta walked into the closed yards, her muscles relaxing as she walked away from her recent prison.

The end of the narrow lane opened onto an island of grass. The main road beyond, which had once played host to hundreds of cars and a constant stream of trams on an hourly basis, now hid under piles of debris. Mature trees with roots sunk deep beneath the city created the impression of a breathing wall that separated her from the carnage. Through the thick bars of their trunks, she could see the hospital beckoning her forward, the street all that separated them.

Trams and cars had met in an agonising snarl of twisted metal and rubber. The dead and the not so dead scattered across the four lanes.

The moans and growls of the infected and the languid buzz of bloated blowflies in the air gave the scene a droning soundtrack that vibrated through her belly. She raised a hand to wave them from her face and pressed back against the wall.

A scuffling at her feet drew her attention. Her eyes fell on a boy, no older than three. He stood near the corner of the brick building, head cocked slightly to the side, milky eyes looking out from an otherwise perfect, emotionless face. Dried snot and flaky tear tracks left shiny trails down mottled cheeks. His arms hung limp from the sleeves of a bloodstained Wiggles T-shirt that had seen happier days. The hem was torn, revealing the greying skin beneath, a ragged, bloodless tear through the abdomen parting to show the fatty viscera beneath. One tiny foot had been bitten off, leaving a stump crawling with larvae.

She coughed as the rancid wind blew the odour of the street directly to her. The noise pulled the dead boy's attention to her sharply.

As the monotonous drone buzzed on, she stared at the still silent, immobile boy. Ignoring her completely, he turned and continued his staggered steps along the wall. She blinked, surprised at the total lack of reaction her presence had prompted.

Stepping away from the wall, she looked past the corner once more, sweeping her gaze along the street. Beyond the tree line, the only cover was the tangled car wrecks and the tram ripped from its tracks. With soft, steady steps, she moved towards the trees. The canopy barely allowed the mottled evening light through, the shade and the tall trunks doing little to hide her from the prowling shadows.

Three steps to her right, a faceless figure swayed slightly, arms askew. An exposed skull topped the swollen body, almost covered by a shroud of insects. It stood between her and the first car that might offer any kind of shelter. It turned stiffly and she watched as it took a step in her direction … before tottering the other way.

It occurred to her then that she was probably not showing the proper reaction one would normally have in this situation. As soon as the thought occurred to her, though, it was labelled as unimportant and brushed aside.

The next was directly behind it, heading towards her as though seeking out her next meal. It too peeled off to amble along the street, not paying the slightest attention to Peta. Her brow creased in confusion, watching as one by one, the creatures' lifeless eyes danced over her position and moved on, none seeming to register her at all. She watched each figure carefully as she slowly walked past them, getting the same reaction each time.

She paused when she reached the car, her temporary refuge allowing her a moment to take in her surroundings. There seemed to be two extremes among the creatures that she could see. The ones that moved freely, passing her with a glance, seemed to be the newer additions to the horde. They showed clearer skin, an almost normal shape where they hadn't been relieved of limbs or chunks of flesh, and seemed to be actively hunting for fresh meat, as much as they could hunt.

The other type seemed rooted to their spot, not walking, barely swaying. These creatures presented a far more gruesome spectacle. The weeks following the initial infection had not been kind. Their legs were bloated and discoloured, their blood pooling in the lowest point turning their feet a puffy, dark purple that gradually faded upwards into a lighter bruised shade. The skin above that was leeched white, in some cases bordering on a sickly yellow. Some had human waste or bloody chunks of flesh coating what was left of their clothes, as wasted muscles released everything they had once held back.

Peta turned her attention back to the notebooks in her hand, wondering distantly if the doctor had gotten this far in his observations. She straightened slightly, turning toward the clinical façade of the hospital across the road.

The automatic doors remained closed as she approached. She knew from her time within the group all power had been routed from the doors to try to sustain the intensive care patients in the hospital. Once they had collectively decided to let them go, the power had been channelled underground, keeping the street level doors securely shut. Her eyes fell on the tiny alley to the side of the building. Within the shadowed recess hid the tiny drain that opened onto the tunnel network below, an entry she had made use of many times when her group went foraging.

She stood slowly; the closest figures to her were the fresher kind. The bright blood smeared around their mouths marked them as having fed recently. Peta clutched the notebooks to her chest, not willing to risk losing them.

Her steps were soft as she moved across the tram tracks and over to the next lane. A flash of movement had her pause, searching out the cause of her distraction. An older man with a heavy backpack stuck his head around the building beside the hospital, sweeping his eyes across the seething street before focusing on the same alley. His eyes drifted over her, not really taking her in at all. She supposed she must have blended in with the listless group, her bloody and spattered clothes, the red streaks that no doubt still coated her face.

Two figures in long sleeves and dark clothes followed him. Each carried a bag that bulged awkwardly on their backs. The smallest trailed slightly. His head was at shoulder height of the young man in front of him, and his nervous glances flashed around more frequently than the others.

Peta remembered her own first foray out into the darker world, the uncertain glances, the jumping at shadows. Silently she urged them forward in her head as she watched their painfully slow progress. The smaller boy's eyes locked with hers. His steps stuttered and he brought up a shaky finger to point at her. His eyes widened and he opened his mouth, grabbing at the boy in front of him and missing by an inch. Peta could see there were three infected close by him, facing the other direction. One peep and they would be all over them. Her mind was torn, half of her was screaming for him to move, to keep his bloody mouth shut and run! The new half, the dominant half that had suppressed her own fear and emotions, seemed content to see how this all played out.

'She …' His voice was silenced as the boy in front realised he had stopped and whirled around to slap a hand over his mouth, his own eyes wide with fear.

For a moment, Peta thought her own experience may not have been isolated, that maybe the threat was ending and they were no longer driven to attack. She scanned the street, looking for any sign that they might have been noticed by the milling throng.

She had the sudden urge to throw something at the wall close to them to see if that would scare a reaction out of either party. The quiet part of her quickly stomped that idea down firmly.

The older man leading them seemed to notice the disturbance in his group. His face adopted an angry flush as he grabbed the boy immediately behind him and thrust him towards the alley. The second boy followed quickly … He hooked a finger in the smallest boy's collar and yanked him forward till he too was in the alley. The movement had the boy stumbling roughly back against the wall.

The city sucked in an anticipatory breath, and released it in an echoing moan that bounced off the walls and oozed through the broken carcasses of cars and people alike as milky eyes turned in unison to find the source of the noise.

Peta could hear the chocked off gasp. The boy's face turned a ghastly grey as he tried to merge with the wall behind him. The man was so close to the boy that he looked like he was chewing on his ear. His hand gripped the front of his shirt tightly and yanked the fabric in a plea for him to move. The boy just shook his head frantically, tiny frantic tremors only betrayed by the slight movement of his hair. The older man's face was contorted; whether in fear or anger, Peta couldn't tell. He kept glancing up, eyes flicking to the nearest infected creature before flitting to the next. The other boy had slipped out of sight down the alley,

A fat, bald man, who appeared to have been a victim of the roads, tottered forward on bloated legs, his fingers snagging the ragged ends of the smallest boy's shirt. The boy gurgled out a scream, paralysed by his terror. The older man gave one last tug before skipping back a step, stumbling over something Peta couldn't see.

The boy he had pushed ahead of him had turned back at the corner, a cry Peta could see forming on his lips was quickly chocked off as the man tackled him with a shoulder to the belly, throwing him over his shoulder and zipping back down the alley.

Peta was left alone to witness the panicked struggles, though she was sure even those who had made it onto the HMAS *Canberra* could hear the gut-wrenching scream. It was soon drowned out by moans as the boy vanished within the throng of hungry corpses.

Peta must have zoned out watching the boy disappearing, piece by piece under clawing hands and teeth. She barely registered her own step forward, taking her from the cover of the cars into the street. She shook her head as if to clear the foggy thoughts that drew her towards the carnage and forced herself to head down the alley after the surviving members of the group. Her gaze swept across the red mess that was revealed as the creatures lost interest and stumbled or crawled away as their remaining limbs allowed.

The creatures continued to ignore her presence as she stepped cautiously towards the alley, the deepening shadows throwing the buildings into sharp contrast. She looked around at the crowded street before following the group behind the stacked up milk crates that hedged the walls. She moved the iron grate that led to the sewers below and lowered herself through to the concrete tomb below.

The tunnel roof was almost obscured by the tubes and pipes that snaked down its length. Sunlight had no hope against the deep shadows, so the main tunnels were lined with battery pow-ered night lights that cast a dim glow. A faint scuffling ahead had her squinting into the blackness. She clutched the notebooks tightly to her chest, ears searching for the slightest suggestion of movement. The scuffle bounced off the walls again, coming from everywhere at once. She gently placed the notebooks on the ground, bringing the hem of her shirt up to scrub at the drying blood on her face. She had too many questions, too many changes about herself since she had been bitten. Something told her that the answer, or something like it, was hidden in the notebooks she picked up and once again clutched against her chest.

Peta followed the pipes down the tunnel; she knew from past use that they led to the main rooms. It didn't take long before she was stopped by an upturned hospital gurney, reinforced with book shelves that almost completely hid the tunnel beyond, save for a narrow, person-sized gap in the middle. A sensor light flashed on, leaving her blinded in the white glare. As her vision returned, a bearded older man swum into view.

He peered at her over his chipped glasses. 'Who are you?'

'Peta Richards. Scavenging team two.' She fell back easily onto the ingrained security questions, though she still eyed the unknown man warily.

'Team two hasn't been on rotation for three weeks,' he shot back, eyes narrowing in suspicion.

Her mouth dropped a little in shock. Three weeks? Had she lost that much time? 'I was … separated from my group.' She was hesitant to say too much about what she had been through, until she got a chance to talk to the HYDRA, and even then she didn't want to tell them too much. As soon as they learned she had been a guest of the depraved doctor, she knew she'd never be trusted again.

The older man looked unconvinced but his shoulders loosened a little. 'You know you will have to go through a full physical, and consent to three days' isolation to prove you're not infected.'

She nodded impatiently, fully aware of the checks they had instituted for this sort of situation. He stepped back, freeing up space for her to climb through. She stepped up onto a milk crate to swing a leg between the bookshelves. She lost her balance and nearly fell forward to the floor, reaching out a hand and grabbing that of the man, who helped steady her on the other side. She squeezed his hand in silent thanks, suddenly overwhelmed with the heady dizziness of relief as she looked back at the wooden wall that stood between her and the hellish tableau outside. Grasping his hand tightly, she pulled him close, planting her lips on his and kissing him deeply before pulling back, shocked at her own behaviour.

'I'm sorry!' she gasped. 'I don't know what came over me! It's just such a relief to be safe again!'

The man flushed a deep red and sputtered out a response before turning and walking briskly down the tunnel ahead of her.

Peta followed closely, a large grin smeared across her face, her five red notebooks clasped tightly to her chest.

Chapter Nine

Hope on the Waves

Thick fingers dropped the handset back into its cradle as a heavy-set man leaned back into his chair with a sigh. It groaned loudly beneath him.

'Gordon!' he barked.

The door behind him opened and a young man, no older than twenty-five, slipped in. He handed Gordon a stack of papers, scratchy handwriting covering the surface. He rubbed his wrist where the pain of handwritten reports seemed to centre.

'Run these to Captain Powell.'

Gordon nodded sharply and slipped out as silently as he had entered. The beefy man stood and ambled over to the small window that looked over the cargo ship they had managed to evacuate to. Echoed calls of his soldiers at work on the decks below drifted up. Highly trained officers working shoulder to shoulder with the grunts to clean up the decks.

There were fewer personnel here than on the boat, and no civilians now—well, *almost* no civilians.

Their doctors had been quick to notice the change in viral patterns, and the orders had been clear enough. No trace of the virus was to remain on board; the risk to humanity was far too great as it was. He scoffed. The higher-ups weren't the ones who had to eliminate the threat. His men would have to live with that on their conscience.

They had tried to keep it to just the infected, then just the ones who had been identified as carriers. After the riot, however, something he blamed mostly on the foreign soldiers on board, the outbreak that had followed had made the effort impossible. A nearby ship had been alerted to the riot and, fearful that this would mean a break in the line, had exaggerated the situation, prompting the captain to fire upon the naval ship. They had evacuated those they could; now, by all official reports, only two civilians remained aboard.

Tired eyes swept over paper littered walls, maps marked and pinned as new orders or updates filtered in. A knock on the door was all the warning he got before Gordon slipped in once more.

'Commander Flint.' He saluted.

The commander nodded, returning the gesture. The end of the world was no reason to slouch on respect and order after all.

'The captain has requested your presence.'

Flint nodded, dismissing him silently. He swept his hat off the back of the chair and stepped through the door the lieutenant held open for him.

The two men walked in silence. Aside from the soldiers working on the deck, the only sound they heard was footsteps and constant sliding as what they managed to salvage was moved around. Their orders had left a notable wound in the morale of the men and they had no idea how to address it.

Gordon rapped sharply on the door and opened it to the quiet command from within. Flint shifted his hat under his arm and walked in.

The captain looked old. Much older than his forty-eight years.

They had served side by side; Flint knew this man better than his own brother, and he knew the onerous task sat heavily on his shoulders. A glance at the commander was all Gordon needed to salute and close the door behind him, leaving the two weary old men alone in the suffocating silence of the captain's room.

'Oh, sit down, man. You've never stood on ceremony with me before. You won't be starting now.'

Flint raised an eyebrow. 'You were wearing the same uniform as me then, sir.' Regardless, he pulled the chair away from the table and sat opposite.

The captain looked at him earnestly, his expression could almost be mistaken for pleading. 'Don't do that. Not you. This is not normal circumstances. This isn't even *remotely* normal.' He lifted a steady hand to his eyes and sighed deeply. 'I'm only captain because they need to be led by someone they know. They need to be able to point to my bars and say "I was just following orders". I'm sure the higher ups are looking for my replacement as we speak. Please don't captain me. I can't do this on my own. It's too much.'

'Richard?' Flint reached out to rest a hand on his friend's shoulder. 'I'm here. I know you have your own orders to follow. This doesn't stop with you.'

'But it *does*, doesn't it?' he bit back. 'I didn't have to give the order. I could have said no.'

'Sure, and you could have let the risk of infection take over the whole ship. I'm not so sure that anyone else in your position would have handled it quite so well.'

'Well? Hundreds of civilians were killed by soldiers under my command. Many of those were not infected.'

Flint winced. Their attempts to keep their attempt at viral

control under the radar had unravelled once their passengers had begun noticing the disappearances. What it had come down to, was 'Is the world worth one hundred lives?' They had been the ones left to answer that question. The fact that every country in the world was invested now, watching closely to see how it was handled, was not doing anything to lessen that responsibility.

Flint cast around for a safer subject to distract the captain. 'I saw the reports on the ground control efforts this morning. According to what they've managed to track, the infection has been confined to within Victorian borders now.'

'Confined is such a pretty word. I prefer culled.'

'It's no different to what we faced here,' Richard hazarded.

'Of course it's different! We're in a confined place, where we had some confirmed cases, panicking civilians, and hot-headed military personnel. We did what we could. Saved what we could. What they're doing is killing. With prejudice. They leave nothing behind them!'

Fear of the virus had led those in charge to encourage a drastic answer to the threat. From what they had heard of the ground orders, no one who survived the first wave of destruction would survive the next.

'Geelong's destroyed, New South Wales has been evacuated to the north, and Horsham's gone.'

Even with the devastation among the Australian army numbers, the additional mix of the world's forces sent to assist in curtailing the threat had been enough to re-enforce the dingo fence, replenish the naval line, and begin the clearance of the southern states. There had been mass evacuations to begin with, but after the first outbreak beyond the safe line had been traced back to an evacuated, seemingly asymptomatic carrier, all bets were off.

Towns were now routinely cleared and burned. Equipment had been brought in to break down any building that might be hiding the virus behind its walls. A viral fire break spread downwards, creeping further each day.

Flint sunk back into his chair, his years pulling at his solid frame. He picked up the hat he had worn so proudly, which now asked so much from him, and flung it against the far wall.

'This is bullshit!' he growled, fingers tearing at the bars on his shoulder, ripping the fabric off with white-knuckled fingers. 'I won't have Banquo's ghostly fingers accusing me of mass murder.' He dropped the tattered fabric to the desk. 'Give me the names of the people wanting out.'

Richard blanched. How did he know? As close as they were, treason was still treason, more so when the safety of the rest of the globe was at stake.

'Relax. I'm not reporting you.'

Richard leaned forward. 'I know some of our men have family out there on the mainland. We'll arrange to pick up who we can and get the fuck out of here. Pitch a tent in Antarctica or something.'

'We're surrounded by Americans, Italians, the fucking Russians, and you think they're just going to let us mosey on in and pick up people they have orders to destroy?'

'No, I don't. Which is why I need those names, soldier.'

Jen blinked in the light as the cupboard she hid in was opened abruptly. Richard held out a hand to help her up.

'What did he want?' Jen asked.

'*He* wanted to meet you.' The voice was behind her, and she spun to face the captain. A ragged tear spoilt the otherwise impeccable uniform. She turned betrayed eyes on Richard, who tried to look reassuring.

'He knows everything.' Richard's hand swept to the desk where a list of names rested. A skim of the first few told her all she needed. She knew if she read further, she would see a list of forty names, mostly Australian soldiers and a few from under other flags. Her name was there, along with Daniel and Jeff, the only civilians remaining on board, though only Jeff and Daniel were listed in any official records.

'There's no need to look so worried. Richard told me you're responsible for getting a few people off the mainland.'

'Not me. I just helped.' She pointed a finger at the name above hers. 'Jeff was responsible for that.'

'Jeff. He's still under guard here, isn't he?' The captain directed the question at Flint.

'He is. They believe either he or Daniel have the coordinates for the larger numbers of refugees on the mainland. They want to make sure they get "special attention".'

'And Daniel?' Jen asked.

'Recovering well.' Richard smiled at Jen. 'He's a smart lad, gives them just enough information to keep them interested.'

Captain Powell nodded and guided Jen down the hall.

'I think introductions might be in order.'

Chapter Ten

The Mountain Refuge

Ruby sat cross-legged, leaning against the rock behind her. Both eyes were tightly shut and her hands rested on her knees. She wasn't meditating. She had never had the patience for that.

Barely a week in to leading her motley crew up into the mountains, she had figured out that if she appeared to be meditating, she could actually get some peace. Apparently the uninitiated thought it was a 'cultural thing'.

She groaned as a soft chime dinged, prompting her to open her eyes. She looked over the haphazard stones that rested against the logs, making up the flimsy outer wall. Two more chimes sounded, and she let out the breath she had been holding, her muscles relaxing slightly.

It had taken several false alarms, and intense re-education for the watch parties at the tender hands of an incredibly frustrated Blue, but they had finally gotten the early warning system working well. She stood and stretched, her knees protesting the movement. Fine boned fingers combed through snow-white hair, plucking a twig out and flicking it to the ground.

'Auntie Ruby!' Her dark-skinned granddaughter skipped up to her, tight curls bouncing on the top of her head. Her clothes had been patched together from countless hand-me-downs, giving her the appearance of a much-loved ragdoll. Everyone's clothes in the camp looked a little like that these days.

'Blue's coming! Ted says he has a boy with him! Can I play with the boy?'

Ruby smiled. Alinga was one of too few children left in the camp now. Somehow they had managed to keep the children mostly innocent of the true horror they faced. She dreaded the day that too was taken from them.

'Let's go meet this boy then.' Ruby reached to take Alinga's smaller hand; the contrast between the girl's smooth fingers and her own weathered, spidery ones made her smile sadly. This was not the legacy she had dreamed she would be leaving her grand-child, and now to have so many relying on her? There was only so much she could teach them.

The two women followed the faintly worn path around rough shelters, nodding a greeting to those they passed. Ruby had been the reason most of the camp community had survived, and even with the outsiders she had earned their respect. She would always be the first person to point out she hadn't done it on her own though. Blue had been her cornerstone after the initial implosion of the group. Now, while she took care of survival and what nat-ural remedies could be found among the rocks, he was in charge of the people in their group, organising the scavenging and watch parties. He had invented the collapsible wall too, their last line of defence against intrusion. Thankfully they hadn't had to use it yet; the narrow path was easy enough to block, providing enough of a hindrance to keep unwelcome guests from entering. Together they made a hell of a team.

Alinga saw them first, squealing as she bounced up on her toes. 'Blue!' she called excitedly, pointing at the kicked up dust where it billowed from the dirt track.

The tired ute grumbled slowly through the gate, a bulky four-wheel-drive crowding in behind it. Ruby frowned. They had made a rule that only the ute was to be used on the mountain. Too many cars drew too much attention. The vehicles crawled to a stop and Ruby moved to Blue's open window, pointedly staring at the big car behind them.

'I'll fill you in, just let us shake the dust off,' said Blue.

He opened the door, and stepped down, just in time to be tackled by a curly beast as Alinga wrapped herself around his legs.

'Hey wombat!' Blue swept her into his arms. 'Where's your mum?'

'Getting mighty tired of sleeping alone.' Eerin, a short woman boasting Alinga's tightly curled hair and Ruby's dark eyes, stepped up behind them. She kissed him lightly on the cheek. 'You're late,' she muttered.

Ruby turned her attention instead to the car behind, subtly allowing them their privacy for a moment.

'If you could tear yourself away from my daughter for one minute,' Blue pulled himself away with some reluctance, 'who is this?'

Eerin asked, 'Where are the others?'

He stepped over to stand beside her. 'This is Andrew, Tracey and Mick. The recent intercepts in town.'

'Not the ones who made radio contact?'

He shook his head. 'There's no radio in the car. It wasn't them.'

She swept speculative eyes over the three tired faces. The man stood in front of his family, back straight, taking in everything in sight. The woman stood a little to his side, one arm slung around the boy's shoulders. She was a fair deal shorter, and every tense muscle screamed distrust. The boy wore the least suspicious look, still a little excited, and far too trusting.

Ruby turned to Blue. 'Unload what you have. Graham and Lou are in the stores. They can log it all in and help you store it. Come find us when you're done and you can fill me on what happened.' She eyed the four-wheel-drive. 'And why *that's* up here.' She crooked a finger at the small family. 'Follow me.'

They walked in a tight group through the thrown up shanty-town. Tents, plywood sheets and corrugated iron were cobbled together in different sized shelters. Alinga danced ahead, a mysteriously acquired chocolate bar in her hand. She stopped at an orange tent where two small boys played.

Ruby led them past where her granddaughter was now sharing her plunder, completely distracted from the newcomers to the camp. She stooped with a wince, entering a plywood structure resting against a thick tree.

Once inside, they were able to straighten a little where the roof sloped up to rest over a low branch. Ruby sat cross-legged on the ground, gesturing for them to follow suit.

'You must love living like this. Your hut looks really nice!' Mick's thoughtless comment earned him a sharp look from his mother.

'Oh yes, I've lived in a hut since I was a child, eating only what we hunted and making clothes from their skins.'

'Really? Wow!' he said, wide eyes raking over the rough walls.

'No. Not really. I had a three-bedroom home on the main street.' she said dryly. 'This is what we threw up till we could sort something more permanent out. That takes time, skills and material. We seem to only have two out of three at any one time. But we have a good system here—everyone contributes to the safety and running of the group. If you're not working in the camp, you participate in the supply runs or the watch parties.'

Andrew frowned. 'Aren't you going to ask what we've been doing? How do you know we can be trusted?'

'Blue is a good judge of character. He wouldn't have allowed you to make it this far if he didn't think you had something to offer. Everyone has done something these days that they're not proud of, experienced something that has left scars. What's past is past.' Ruby didn't mention that they would still be under close supervision for the first few weeks. 'This here is a communal hut—you'll notice that the family huts are a lot smaller. I'll show you to one of those shortly.' She stood up, stretching out her back. 'Autumn will be here soon, and the temperature will drop. Keep this in mind when you're thinking of how to fix up your hut. We'll make another few runs to gather what we need, so take note of anything you want to try to collect and tell either Blue or me.'

They filed out once more into the organised chaos of wood, plastic and iron. Ruby nodded at some of the faces that had appeared, checking out the newcomers. As they walked, she pointed out with more than a little pride their water collection and the solar panels that gave them what little power they used. Rock walls surrounded them on two opposite sides; at the far edge between them it dropped off in a steep cliff, impossible for the uncoordinated shamblers below. The cliff also provided their last avenue of escape. Secured ropes were flung over the side, ready to use at a moment's notice. This left only one side, the hard to access track, now mostly blocked off by the collapsible wall. Ruby kept the security features to herself, recent events having taught her a valuable lesson in caution.

The people they passed were tired, their losses evidenced by the grief on their unwashed faces. Far too few, even for the small town below. What remained of the families huddled together in their twos and threes, but many were alone. Sorrow and loss were still clear on their faces.

The lean-to Ruby led them to was made mostly of corrugated iron. A flimsy plastic sheet was flung over the top to keep the rain out. It barely reached midway up Andrew's chest.

Ruby glanced at them from the corner of her eye. She could see them sizing up the minute space.

'We try to encourage people to spend time together in the community spaces. Relationships need to be strong if we are to trust each other. That's why we built the bigger hut we were in before. We eat outside unless the rains kick up, we try to keep our spirits up on our down time.' She hesitated before adopting a more serious tone. 'I'm sure Blue told you that we lost half our group. Those who left stayed somewhat isolated from the group for the most part beforehand. It's a mistake we have no desire to repeat.'

'That doesn't leave a lot of privacy,' Tracey was quick to point out.

'If you find yourself in need of privacy,' she grinned, 'there are places a little further from camp. Fair warning though, everyone knows what they're used for.' A wry eyebrow lifted knowingly.

A light chime heralded an engine as it rumbled to life behind them. They turned to see what Ruby knew would be the beat-up ute backing up slowly through the gap in the fence.

'It's time for the next watch,' Ruby explained, not even glancing to the front.

Blue had honed the watches to a fine art, the resting group handing over what had happened and who was stationed where. Those who had been left behind and any injured were sent to J Ward. The only watch that never changed over was Steve, their second line of defence. His wheelchair wouldn't allow him further than the incoming road, but they had managed to turn his camper into a road block positioned halfway to the mountain. The watch going out to the town dropped his portion of rations off before moving on.

The camp, the town, the quarantine and the checkpoints were in constant communication with each other, relaying even the most trivial of information to assure the others of their safety and lack of incoming threat.

Ruby could see Blue approaching with her daughter, neither looking particularly happy. Blue's fingers toyed with a book she recognised all too well. She turned to the new family to excuse herself. 'The cooks will have dinner ready soon. I'll leave you to settle in. Tomorrow we'll discuss where you can contribute in the camp.' She smiled softly, not waiting for an answer as she moved away.

'The camp watch picked up some radio chatter about military action up north,' Eerin began as they headed towards the communal hut.

Blue pulled a small case near the door to the centre of the room and pulled a map from within to rest on the top. The map was a full map of Australia, large enough to curl limply over the edges, like it had melted in the summer heat. A red line ran from the centre of South Australia, through the desert till it met the coast just below Canberra. Several more lines crept ever closer to where they were camped, some dipping in dramatically where the population was sparser. Several towns had the word 'silent' scrawled over the top.

'From the sounds of it, a few survivors saw something up here.' Eerin tapped a finger on a spot little more than a kilometre from the northern edge of the mountains.

Blue flipped the notebook open, the last radio transcript scrawled across its pages, reading it silently.

'Three trucks. Maybe fifty soldiers? They've just left now. It looks like they've cleared the town.'

'Is anyone left?'

'Not that we can make out. We didn't see anyone leave though. Could they have all been wiped out beforehand?'

'Doubtful. The last crew we heard from said they were well fortified, just like the others. No chance of accidental break through.'

'Shall we move closer? Take a look?'

'Do that. Just a quick look. No moving in till I say so.'

There was a slight gap, then the writing came back, messier, panicked.

'They're dead! They're all dead!'

'Were they sick?'

'They looked normal. If they were sick, the military must have a new early detection method. There were no bites, no sign of infection that we could see.'

'Come back. We'll send in a team to get whatever's left.'

'It goes silent after that. It's not a group we've attempted to make contact with before, and we can't reach anyone that we have been speaking to above the last line.' Blue's face was devoid of his usual humour. 'What if they're not checking for infection anymore? What if they're just wiping people out?'

Eerin shushed him, glancing around quickly. 'That's how panic starts. Let's not let that little rumour take root.'

Blue jabbed a finger at the map. 'They're getting closer! They're right on our doorstep! When do you think we should do something about this?'

Ruby rested a hand on both of their shoulders.

'We don't know that the town wasn't infected,' she stated calmly. 'All we have to go on is the word of an unknown source.'

She squeezed Blue's shoulder when it was evident he wanted to voice his own objection.

'That doesn't mean we won't take steps here,' Ruby said. 'Let's double the guards and post a few further out. We'll tell the camp that restriction of all unnecessary noise is the rule until further notice. They can draw their own conclusions. Radio the watches in town though; they need to be aware that there's a possibility perceived friendly forces may not be approachable. We'll take a wait-and-see approach for now.'

'I don't like this,' Blue bit out. 'The signs of infection are obvious. You can't mistake healthy for dead. There's something going on.'

Ruby sighed. 'I know, but we can't make a move until we have confirmation. The military is still our biggest hope of getting out of here. I won't destroy the hope of evacuation just yet.'

'What exactly are you saying, Blue?' Eerin hissed. 'You both sound like you think the military is heading up some huge conspiracy to kill everyone just to hide what's going on!' The slight hysteria in her voice had Blue pulling her towards him.

'I think at this point we can't rule that out,' Ruby said softly, tapping the red lines closing in on them.

'You're being ridiculous. How could they hide the mass killing of the entire eastern seaboard from the world?' Eerin said. 'They'd never get away with it!'

'How many people die from diseases every day?' Blue reasoned. 'How many new diseases are found that don't have a cure? They would find it easy to invent something that came over to our shores that we weren't prepared for. Any news that managed to get out would be laughed off as a hoax and forgotten in less than a month. Seriously, sweetheart, who would believe in zombies?'

Chapter Eleven
Hide and Seek

James looked around warily. They had stopped in the shadow of a supermarket, watching as Joe peeked around the corner of the building. The ex-soldier held up a finger, waited a moment, and waved the small group forward.

They hadn't spoken more than a word at a time since they left the truck, relying instead on rough signals.

The building overlooked a large car park serving the supermarket and surrounding shops, easily holding at least five hundred cars. It was packed now. The baking sun reflected off the glass panes, blinding them from several directions at once.

The air was thick with the stench of rot, building on top of the already ripe smell they had acclimatised to.

Karen gagged, covering her nose and mouth. James took a deep breath, feeling his throat close in an attempt to protect his lungs. Saliva pooled in his mouth as bile churned in his empty stomach. He fought through it, taking another deep breath and another. Eventually it became a little easier, the stench losing some of its edge as he forced himself to get used to it.

The only people who seemed to be completely unaffected by the almost visible stench moved slowly between the parked cars, their guttural groans bouncing off the walls around them.

It was more than the normal stink that usually curled off the unwashed corpses. This was folded in with the odour of rotten meat, and month-old produce that wafted from the doors of the grocery store at the end of the car park.

'We're about two blocks away from the main road,' Joe murmured, stepping back into the group. 'We can either go around the car park, which takes us far too close to the store for my comfort, or through it.' He sounded exhausted, a sentiment that was reflected off each face around him. They had been looking for any sign of habitation in the labyrinthine streets of the town, breaking through overgrown gardens, stepping over dead pets and trying to avoid the live ones. So far they were met only with disappointment. It seemed that whatever was left of the living people meant to stay hidden.

'We don't even know where to look!' James was starting to feel despondent as time and grief pulled at him. 'Are we even going in the right direction?' He turned pleading eyes on Joe.

So far they had followed Joe unquestioningly, willing to let his experience guide them. If James was beginning to question the futility of an exercise though, it was a safe bet he was not alone.

Joe turned his head and nodded across the car park to the buildings that shadowed the other side.

'We might be closer than you think. Something tells me these things don't care about rubbish control.' Barely visible above the throng, the building he nodded to was bordered with a pile of trash, heaped along one side.

'You couldn't have known that was there,' Karen reasoned. 'How did you know to come in this direction?'

'I followed the crowd,' he stated simply. 'We didn't have much to go on, so I figured that if there were a number of people living in one area, the smell or the sound, *whatever* it is that pulls these bastards in, would act as a magnet. I hoped we might find our own signs of life as we got closer.'

'And a rubbish tip is your sign of life?'

'A rubbish tip outside the courthouse is more than we had to go on before. Plus, it seems quite popular.' The crowds did indeed seem to be pulled the place, growing thicker closer to the building.

'Is it just the courthouse?' Karen squinted against the glare. 'Isn't the theatre over there too?'

'Does it matter?' Joe asked. 'We have something to go on. Either one could have possibly been turned into liveable quarters.'

'So what now?' Karen asked.

'We find a way in.' James, his faith renewed slightly, felt energised again. The thought that his daughter, the last of his family, could be mere blocks away had him all but bouncing in place.

'It might not be that simple,' Joe warned. 'The guys that took the camper were violent criminals. One would think that people in charge of a town in an emergency would be the authorities. Something went wrong here.'

'No, it really is that simple,' James insisted. 'They have my daughter. I'm going into that building to get her.'

'I'm not disputing that. We will do everything we can to get her back.' Joe fought to keep his voice low as he spoke over him. 'But we have to do it carefully.'

'What if there was a way to get in without having to go through the car park?' Karen spoke up. 'This is a gold mine city—there are mines and tunnels all through it! I'm pretty sure both the courthouse and the theatre are old enough to have an underground cellar or drains or something. I know there used to be a creek that ran in front of the courthouse until they built over it. I'm pretty sure it runs underneath now, not so much a creek though, more like storm-water drainage.'

Joe seemed to mull it over. 'If these guys are as regular with their patrols as they sounded, it makes sense that they would have a way out of the building that doesn't lead them into that mess.' He gestured towards the crowd again. 'Chances are there is another way out. If there wasn't something before, there probably is now.' He glanced towards Karen. 'Do you know how to get into the storm drain?'

'I think so. I mean, I've heard people talk about it, but I haven't been there myself.' She pointed to a tree shaded area. 'There's a ditch under the trees there.'

Joe moved in the direction she pointed, the rest of the group following quietly.

James glanced back at the courthouse; he was sure his tension was obvious to the others. Alex had moved a little closer to his son, trying to offer support where he could.

They stopped at the edge of the concrete-lined channel. The trees provided a patchy shadow that deepened where it vanished under the road towards the courthouse.

Joe dropped over the side, raising a hand to help Karen over the side to join him.

'If this is the Yarrowee River,' she brushed her hands down her pants down nervously, her voice muted by the mossy bricks that surrounded them, 'it should take us right under the courthouse.'

Joe took the lead once more. Feet lifted a little higher than normal and were placed with an almost exaggerated care on the drying moss. The mouth of the tunnel before them was like a hungry mouth. Distant moans echoed off the dark walls.

Joe didn't glance back as he stepped into the shadows, the others keeping their eyes facing forward as they followed close behind.

As James entered the tunnel, the darkness seemed to growl at their intrusion. His hand shot out, fumbling fingers catching on fabric close by and he grabbed hold firmly. A Joe-ish grunt was the only assurance he got that his hand hadn't found a set of chomping teeth. Behind him, fingers grabbed at his own shirt. His heart stuttered momentarily before remembering the last two members still behind him.

James sucked in a breath as Alex leaned over his shoulder, breath hot in his ear. 'It's pitch black. How are we supposed to find our way in the dark?'

His whispered question caught Joe's ears, his shirt twisting a little in James's fingers as he turned slightly. 'Keep to the sides,' he whispered back.

The shadows had already begun to give way, showing some definition as their eyes adjusted to the lack of light. James could see Joe's ghostly hand stretched out to rest against the wall beside him.

'If Karen is right, the drain should take us right under the courthouse. We'll keep going until we hear something above us.'

James couldn't help the eye roll. The hair-raising growls were coming from everywhere! The idea that they would be able to identify any noise above them was laughable. He kept those unhelpful thoughts to himself though, and they inched their way along in silence. The noise was an indecipherable mess of tangled notes, meshing together to create one rolling growl that gave the impression of something much larger waiting just ahead. Behind him, Karen's hand shook slightly where it gripped his shirt. His own fingers were slightly numb where they curled into Joe's. He stumbled as Joe paused in his steps.

'What? Why are we stopping?' Alex hissed from the back.

Joe's head was tilted towards the ceiling. James craned his head back to look. A thin, barely noticeable outline of a square hatch overhead barely glinted off the narrow handholds inset into the mossy brick walls.

'I think we found it,' James whispered over his shoulder, moving aside slightly as Alex stepped up beside him. 'The back door. Should we knock?'

'Let's not,' Alex muttered dryly.

Joe reached up to grab the first handhold, yanking on it once before looking back at the group, and stepping up.

One by one, they made their way up the tentative ladder, testing each grip as they came to it. Joe froze suddenly, three grips from the top. He stooped low towards James, barely a grip from his heel.

'The holds are safe, but there seems to be a wire just over the last one. I can't see where it connects to, but try not to hit it.'

James looked back to pass it on, but the nods from Alex and Karen reassured him that they had heard Joe's instruction.

Joe reached up, pushing slightly on the boards above his head. They gave way easily, allowing a soft light to spill down around them, highlighting the iron bars they clung to. For a second, James saw Joe clearly as he peered into the room above. He flinched, head ducking low as Joe pulled the hatch down again, cutting the light off once more. He could barely make out the hissed 'Shit!' over the grind of wood and stone as the cover was lifted once again. A torch beam danced over their faces, blinding them completely. James hid his face in his arm.

'Who the hell are you?'

It was a female voice, young by the sound of it.

'Uh … Avon calling?' James quipped. His natural defence of cracking jokes to alleviate tension had Joe spinning to glare at him.

Joe turned back to the girl, holding his free hand up to show he was unarmed. He took in her dirty, frightened face, the unsure glances to the door behind her as she kept her voice low. She still hadn't called for help. He took the chance.

'Some of our group were taken. We think they might be here.'

Something flashed over her face, too quick for him to decipher. She seemed to be in two minds, clearly warring with her choice of action. Placing the torch on the floor, she beckoned them up quickly.

'Watch the trip wire,' she cautioned. 'Quickly!'

They hoisted themselves from the hole, falling into a tangle of sprawling limbs as she tried to hurry them up. The girl was fidgety, glancing towards the door as she twisted her fingers anxiously.

'I'm Magda.' She flitted over to the desk, pawing through paperwork. 'I think I know who you're talking about—they brought someone back with them on the last raid. She was saying something about tr …' She seemed to think better about what she was saying. 'There was a girl with them, a baby.'

James's head shot up, eyes sharp.

'It's not going to be easy to get them out, but I can help.'

Joe's eyes narrowed in sudden suspicion. 'Why would you help?'

She looked at him like she was questioning his sanity. 'Do you think you're the only ones these guys have screwed over? We were fine till they showed up! Sure, we were shook up and grieving, but we were fine! They came in, saw an opportunity, and took it. Now my father—*all* the surviving men—are locked up in the jailhouse. Everyone else they've kept here, under watch. We're hostages in our own town.' She sucked in a deep breath. 'I'll help you get your people out, if you help me get mine.'

Joe and Alex exchanged unsure glances. This was quickly getting out of hand. From a simple rescue, they were treading dangerously close to a small-scale revolution.

'Sure,' James blurted out. If you help us get Charlie out, we'll help you.'

'James …' Alex murmured cautiously.

'Deal.' Magda was quick to agree, holding a small hand out to shake.

Karen looked warningly at the older men, clearly siding with James on this matter. Joe hung his head in defeat.

'Fine.' Magda's face lit up. 'What's your plan?'

A door slammed further down the corridor. Magda blanched. 'Hide!' she hissed. 'No not there!' She herded them away from the hatch Karen had been stooping to open. 'It's a patrol. Go behind the boxes!'

They had barely made it, and scarcely fit. Magda stood firmly in front of the boxes, clipboard in shaking hand, just as the door swung open. The first man barely spared her a glance, then four other men filed in behind him, each holding a rifle. One swept his eyes up and down her slight form, leering a little.

'Knock it off, Tim. The younger ones are off limits.' The first man didn't even glance up as he spoke.

James could feel Karen tensing beside him.

The man pulled out something that looked like a phone. 'The markers are at seventy kilometres. This is a point and tag mission.

Just plant the markers. *Don't* take them out. This is for the trackers.' He eyed each man in his small group, lingering on Tim. 'Don't fuck it up.' He hoisted up the wooden hatch. One by one the men vanished below.

As the last man cleared the hatch, and the wooden cover slid back home with a breathy *thunk*, Joe led them out once more.

'What were they talking about, "trackers"?'

Magda hesitated, but seemed to talk herself into an explanation. 'They must have found something after they came back with the new people. Some of the dead people had collars on them, and they found something that could track them. One of them said it was a government project.'

'Government?' Joe asked, puzzled. 'Where would they have had time to …' He broke off, confusion sweeping over his face. 'Helena?'

Chapter Twelve
Purpose

The room had once been an office in a row of offices, taking up the upper level of the decommissioned courthouse. The fittings were cobbled together and mismatching in a way that clashed violently, stolen from houses and hotels nearby. The garish bedspread Helena sat on was nearly obscured by the spread of parts from miscellaneous computer fragments. She turned the small GPS over in her hand. Small clusters of red dots were scattered across the screen. In the centre of the screen, the area identifying the courthouse was almost swallowed by a sea of red. A laptop rested on the floral patterned cover beside her, open to a near indecipherable matrix of code.

'Done … I think,' she said to the empty room. Her eyes fell on Charlie, sleeping on the floor in a pile of cushions. 'Not that you care, but I've managed to replicate a very advanced piece of machinery with little more than jewellers' tools and whatever these baboons have managed to filch from the nearby shops. Quite the accomplishment if I do say so myself.'

'The *baboons* would like me to tell you they placed the markers you asked for and the next group has been sent to place the last lot.' Magda closed the door softly behind her. 'And I'd like to point out how lucky you were that it was me who walked in to hear that.'

Helena scoffed. 'And what do you think they would do if they did hear me? They need me. They can't make the trackers work otherwise.'

Magda hesitated; each time she had asked, Helena had danced around the answer. Now with the newcomers she had hidden downstairs, she felt the need to ask again. 'The men said something about the trackers being a government project. How did you know how to make the same computers?'

'It's not exactly the same computer.' She smiled evasively. 'It's better now.' She handed over the small GPS when Magda looked at it quizzically, resigned to the fact that again she wouldn't have her question answered. 'I've managed to link the new trackers now. When they're close to others, the signals connect to show where greater numbers are. The more trackers, the bigger the dot. Not only that …' She excitedly pulled the laptop onto her lap. '… I've tweaked it a little to pick up on ambient noise and show the increase as the green circle! Because the predominant ambient noise is moans and groans, it will show the unmarked hordes that the individual creatures move into. I call it …' she held her hands up dramatically, '… the Locust.'

Magda looked blankly at the GPS unit in her hand.

Helena narrowed her eyes. 'You're usually a lot more interested in these things. What happened?'

Magda shifted uneasily, her eyes dancing to the sleeping toddler in the corner of the room. 'We had a few visitors, and they were asking about you two. Three men and a woman.'

'Where are they now?'

'I hid them in one of the smaller side rooms. I don't know how to get them up here without anyone noticing.'

Helena was already eyeing the room to see what she would

need to take. She closed the laptop, reassuring herself mentally that it would be easier this way.

'Pass the bag, please?'

Magda handed her a backpack that Helena promptly turned upside down, spilling piles of gadgets and discarded parts onto the floor. She slid the laptop in, closing the zip. She would likely be greatly disadvantaged without the electricity she had here, but she had survived before. 'Can you carry th— Charlie, please?'

'There's one more thing,' Magda said, not meeting Helena's eyes. 'I may have told them I'd take them to you in return for them helping us get rid of the bikers.'

Her words were mumbled, but Helena heard them clearly.

Magda paled a little at the dark look Helena shot her. 'I had to!'

'No you didn't.'

'How else am I going to help my dad?'

'It's an unnecessary risk. You know the odds that they've survived until now.'

The girl teared up. 'He's alive! I know it!' As quick as it had come, the fight drained from her. 'I'm sorry. I saw an opportunity and jumped at it. You would have done the same.'

'Go get what you need. One way or another, we're not coming back here.'

Magda darted out the door. Helena could hear her light footsteps down the corridor to the other rooms. She slipped out another GPS unit, this one modified for her specifications alone. Her thumb depressed the button on the side.

'South Base, do you copy?'

'*We read you, Mouse.*'

'My ride's here, but my guide insists on a detour. I'll be headed out of the city soon.'

'Report when you're clear. Head down here to South Base as soon as you can.'

'Copy that. Have we heard from the north?'

'North has been compromised by an outside party. We've been ordered to maintain our current course until the situation is brought under control.'

She growled softly. 'Understood. Have you heard from the city?'

'We believe the doctor is compromised. All contact has been lost.'

She was silent for a moment. Unhinged though he was at times, Dr Marcus had been an intelligent and innovative colleague. Hopefully, his loss would not have too great an impact on their project.

'Understood. I'll be in contact when I'm clear.'

'Copy that. Out.'

The unit fell silent in her hand. Her plans beginning to take shape, she slipped off the bed, crouching in front of Charlie.

'Well, we've had a few rough patches, but we're near the end now. You and I are going to change the world.' She slung the backpack over her shoulder; the bag thumped against the back of her knees where it hung comically low.

Magda opened the door once more. 'The men who stayed back have been drinking fairly heavily, so we might be all right. They had me hauling drinks in since the last group left. The only ones not drinking are the guys who came back last. They're still sleeping.'

'Right. Grab Charlie. Let's see if her daddy's thought of a plan.' She moved through the door and glanced into the corridor. 'Where are they drinking?'

'In the foyer. We'll have to go straight past them.'

They made slow progress. Magda stayed close to Helena, Charlie tight in her arms. With one group out, and the remaining men asleep, or at least less than coherent, they were probably showing more caution than strictly necessary. Regardless, they held their tongues as they entered the rear stairwell.

Magda pushed the final door open, leading them out into the last hallway. She slipped into a near room and came out, pushing a waiter's cart, already well stocked with beer. She crouched down to Helena's height. 'Stay behind the doorway. With luck, they'll be too distracted with the beer. I'll be out as soon as their focus is on that.'

Helena could do little more than nod, taking Charlie and letting Magda step past and into the room. Soused cheers tumbled through the entrance, and she could hear pushing as the men tousled to reach the new distraction, almost piling onto the cart. A high-pitched yelp preceded a tiny dog that raced through the doorway into Helena's path. It bared its sharp teeth, growling sharply when it saw them.

'What the hell is wrong with the bloody dog?' The slurred words bellowed.

Magda stood quickly, gesturing for Helena to stay out of sight behind the trolley. Rough hands grabbed at the cart as a huge shadow cast them into darkness. Helena smothered Charlie's cry with her hand as the rough handling jolted them back. Magda quickly stood between him and the cart, fixing a fake smile on her face.

'I'll bring it in. You go sit down, sir.' The shadows moved with a laugh and Helena could see a meaty hand come down hard on the fragile shoulder.

'You have one with me,' he mumbled, pulling her to him.

She shifted again, this time pushing the cart a little closer to the other side of the entrance. The dog moved too. Its sharp barks still threatened to alert the rest of the men to the escapees.

'Shaddup.' The bulky shadow aimed a kick at the dog, missing by a mile as he stumbled. 'Le's go. Beer. Now.' He grabbed her arm, pulling her into the room with a yelp before reaching back to grab at the trolley.

Magda laughed a little too shrilly, pushing the uncoordinated hand off. 'I can't, sir. I have to run a few errands for Mr King still.' She walked quickly out the door, safe from the drunken groping by the trolley she deftly kept between them.

Helena moved quickly, hidden by the trolley. As soon as Magda joined them, Helena threw the combined weight of Charlie and herself at the still yapping dog, which danced to the side. Magda stumbled, accidentally grabbing at Charlie, who let out her own squalling mew of discomfort.

'Wassat?'

'Just the bloody dog.'

'Sound like a kid t' me.'

Helena held her breath as the soggy words drew closer. The only thing that offered cover was a large pot plant on the far side of the hall. Magda grabbed her shirt, pulling her to a door on the other side of the hall and flinging it open.

'Come on!' She pushed the shorter woman in, the dog bounding in excitedly on their heels. 'Oh hell! They'll be looking for the damn mutt!' she said, pressing an ear against the door to listen for the inevitable footfalls.

There was a slide*thump* and the dog yelped, then silence.

Helena spun to face the deeply shadowed room. The pale light of the open window provided a perfect backdrop for the tall shape that wavered in front of it. She backed up against the door, pressing Magda and Charlie against it.

'Baby?' The shadow moved towards them unsteadily.

'Da!'

'Shh!'

'Oh God, is it them?'

The dark room was a flurry of hushed activity as hands grabbed at people, a torch swept over long lost faces. Charlie launched towards James's arms, and Magda leaned uncertainly against the wall, suddenly empty-handed.

It wasn't surprising that in the excitement nobody noticed the door swing open. Magda squawked and fell into Helena as the door pushed her forward.

'Wha' th' fu—' The garbled words were cut off as Alex pulled the man in and smacked a fist into his nose. He fell noisily, pulling over a chair from against the wall as he fell senseless to the ground.

'They'll have heard that,' Joe growled, kicking the man sharply when he moaned a little.

'Can we use the window?' Karen asked, glancing through the dirty glass.

'Is the dog still out there?'

'You threw the dog through the window?' Magda snorted.

'I panicked!' James defended from Charlie's neck.

Karen cracked the window open again. 'It's not a far drop, and, lucky us, the dog bolted away and distracted the less than lively citizens. They're still out there, but facing the wrong way. As long as we stay low, the hedge should hide us.'

Footsteps behind the door made the decision for them and Joe jumped to the ground, helping Karen after him. One by one, they dropped to the grass below. James passed Charlie through to his father before helping Helena down and following suit.

The door crashed into the wall as it was slammed inwards. James ducked out of habit, pressing himself against the wall.

'Go!' he hissed, sliding along the wall, his attention riveted on the half-chewed woman that had started to move in their direction. 'Move!'

Magda led them to a pile of boxes that were hurriedly pulled aside to reveal a storm drain. Alex pushed her firmly aside to pull up the heavy grate, cringing as iron grated on concrete. One by one, they tumbled into the dark, cramped pipe.

'What is this?' All James could make out in the thin light that filtered through was the solid concrete walls curving around them. A few metres up the shadows thinned again, then there was nothing but darkness.

'I've had to hide here several times. The pipes run along the service tunnel between the prison and the courthouse.' Magda crouched by the wall, feeling around on the damp ground before standing with a triumphant squeak. In her hand was a small crank-up torch, the cartoon on the side doing nothing to hide the cheapness of the product. There was a dozen or so whirring cranks and a thin, reedy light sputtered into life.

'I got your kid back to you. You said you would help us.' Magda's firm words sounded less threatening than a puppy crying to get in, and curled off into a whine at the end. She huddled in on herself, small and uncertain, and so painfully alone.

'We might have an idea. It depends on what you can tell us of the security and layout of the place.'

'Oh, plenty! I have to take the food to the prisoners.' Her face lit up, then dimmed a little. 'The bikers keep the key on them though. There are always guards in the gate room.'

James nodded, having already assumed this.

Alex leaned forward a little, keeping his voice low to reduce the carry. 'What can you tell us about the king?'

Chapter Thirteen

Into the Valley

Blue squinted into the evening glare. After the lighter atmosphere of the camp, the interior of the ute was pressingly silent, matching the dour streets he manoeuvred through.

Narrowed eyes carefully swept the road ahead. Even as an Ararat native, he was sure he had never known these roads as intimately as he did now. The cheery orange glow of the streetlights greeted him in the distance as he left the leafy tunnel that hid the road from sight.

He coasted to a stop at the blockage in the road ahead. The motorhome reached over both lanes, cutting off access to anyone without a four-wheel-drive.

The door opened, spilling light around the spokes of a wheelchair, the shadow of a shotgun resting across its occupant's knees. Blue cracked his window a little, not wanting to climb out without making sure he had been recognised.

'Quiet night, Steve?'

'Blue? Geez, I could have shot you. You're back so soon?'

Blue shrugged absently. 'How're things here?'

'Quiet, thank God. You taking watch again?'

'Yeah.' Blue sighed. 'Heading up to J Ward now.'

'You know if Tam's still up there?'

Blue winced. If the kid turned, there was no way he could do what he needed to with her there.

'I'll have Damien bring her back if it needs doing. Have you heard how he's doing?'

'He hasn't woken up yet, but the fever seems to be absent from what I've heard. A bit of infection, so we'll have to see how he is when he wakes up. Gwen popped in to see him before she headed up to camp not half an hour ago, said he should be fine. Ivan's taken over at the clinic.'

Blue felt a smile tease the ends of his moustache at the news. A day where he didn't have to shoot an injured kid was a good day in his book.

'I'll send Damien past with your supplies.' He thumped the roof of his ute in farewell and wound the window up again.

Steve closed the door, the motorhome shifting back just enough to allow the ute through before rolling back into position behind him.

By the time Blue got to J Ward, everyone should know he had checked in, from the high camp to the clinic. The constant communication was what kept them safe and alert from any threat from the city side of the mountain.

He parked before the tall, stone walls of the prison for the criminally insane and swung the door open just as Damien appeared at the main doors.

'How are they?' Although he had no doubt Steve had told him what he knew, Blue made it a habit to ask again in case anything had changed. The right side of Damien's mouth ticked up into a grin and he nodded.

Blue's breath huffed out in relief. 'Before you swing past Ivan for Steve's supplies, you might need to round up some gas. I'll send

Tam out—go get some rest.' Damien looked tired and closed his eyes as he took the driver's seat, head falling back onto the headrest.

Blue didn't need to go far; Tameka sat pouting inside the second door.

'They kicked me out. I wasn't even making noise!'

Blue held a hand out. She grabbed it and he hauled her up.

'You need your rest too. I'll keep watch here—you can come back in the morning.' These days it was easy to forget that she and Caleb were still kids at sixteen. 'Damien's waiting. He'll need your help more than Caleb does at the moment.'

Still not happy to be sent back to camp, she frowned but left, joining Damien in the car.

Left alone in the tiny foyer, Blue picked up the candle that was all they allowed for light this close to the entrance. It did little to dispel the gloom as he walked around the staircase to the last door that led out to the gardens.

It swung open silently, revealing turned up soil where manicured grass once stood before the main cell blocks. Now acting as a community garden for three separate camps, it was one of their proudest accomplishments. The ramp clanked softly under his feet, and a light flickered in an upstairs room to the left. The door opened before he reached it. Kat, one of the many live-in carers, let him in silently. He nodded in thanks, both faces bathed in the dim glow of the candle.

He found Caleb in the first cell, unconscious, his arms loosely bound in a straitjacket. It was standard precaution for those under quarantine. His injured leg was unfettered, easy to keep an eye on, and his brow was thankfully still clear of fever sweat as he slept easily under Gwen's sedation. He shut the door softly and stepped into the kitchen.

Kat had already started making coffee, her back to him as she worked. He took the cup thankfully and leaned back in a chair. Kat poured her own cup and flipped her book open to read.

Despite being desperately tired, Damien couldn't sleep. He sat on a lower branch of the tree, looking back into the camp, fingers toying with the rope to his left that held the collapsible wall in place. Something was pinging at his nerves.

Tameka had crawled into her tent and presumably fallen asleep as he hadn't seen so much as a twitch from her. He wasn't surprised; she had dozed off twice in the car on the way up.

The snap of a twig in the darkness had him clutching at the cricket bat resting beside him. They still got the occasional kangaroo and plenty of rabbits around here, and it had been a while since one of the infected had gotten this close. Still, better safe and all that.

'Who's there?' He kept his voice low, scanning the trees for movement. A shape stumbled forward, the bright Hawaiian shirt kicking at a distant memory.

'Trish?' Ruby's sister had been wearing that shirt the night she left with most of the group. 'What are you doing back? Ruby's going to kill you if she sees you.'

She walked towards him, stepping into the reflected camp light that bounced off the trees.

'You really shouldn't …'

Her eyes came up to meet his, the tell-tale film of infection evident even in the low light.

'Oh. Damn.'

He brought the bat up to his shoulder, eager to dispatch her before Ruby could see what had happened. He stepped forward and swung upwards, the bat colliding with a wet snap.

Damien stepped forward to finish the job, faltering when a heavy hand landed on his shoulder, pulling him off balance.

He flailed wildly, managing to maintain his grip on the bat by his fingernails. He twisted wildly, trying to thrust the bat between them, wedging it below its chin. Sharp teeth found his calf, digging in deep. He let out a pained bellow.

There was shuffling in the direction of the camp, and more behind him. Through the trees, he could barely make out shifting shapes heading towards the sleeping camp.

Numbly, he reached out towards the tree, fingers finding the rope he had been playing with only moments before. He yanked it, hard.

At first, he was worried nothing had happened. Then the rumbling started; pebbles at first, then the crack of huge limbs that had been released. The weight of the rocks behind it would help in pushing the logs downhill before they threw themselves forward. There was enough weight and energy pent up in that wall to take out most of the threat he could see here. With a smile, he watched the wall collapse right on top of him.

Ruby watched in horror as the wall crumbled, burying Damien in a tomb of rock and wood. The heavy wave took down the smaller trees completely and threw rocks with a deafening crash down through the gorge.

The whole camp ran to investigate the ruckus. Mick moved up to stand beside Ruby, his eyes wide. Tracey stood behind him, her hand fluttering in front of her mouth in shock.

Among the unstable logs, Ruby could still see things moving. Not many thankfully—the wall had done its terrible duty well. She seizing up a shovel as she tiptoed across the nearest log and buried the bladed end into the head of a woman reaching up towards her. Not hesitating, she scrambled onwards. Movement behind her told her the others were following her lead.

She saw a fully woken Tameka leap ahead, a hatchet in hand, crouching to deliver a sharp thwack to the head of a man in purple, putting him out of his misery. Ruby glanced behind at Tracey's sharp 'No!', seeing Andrew try to press a knife into his son's hand and his mother pushing him behind her metaphorical skirts.

Ruby stopped her press onwards and walked back, slapping the overprotective woman sharply and pushing her shovel into the boy's hand. She guided him towards Andrew and stood in front of a shocked Tracey.

'I understand that you want to protect him, but you need to understand that time has passed. He needs to learn to protect himself. You won't always be there, and what will happen the minute you're not? If he can't defend himself, make no mistake, your boy will die.'

Tracey stood speechless for the first time since Ruby had known her, her hand pressed against the reddening mark on her cheek. Tracey glanced to the new clearing. Ruby stood with her, watching as many of the refugees picked their way across unstable logs, stopping here and there to finish someone off. Mick and Andrew were along the tree line now, Mick letting Andrew show him how to finish one off quickly.

'Perhaps he'll make it through this, perhaps most of us will. Many will die though, and those who can't rely on their own instincts will be among the first to go.'

Tracey spun on her heel, vanishing into the tent. Ruby sighed in frustration. She was running out of ideas with that woman.

A moment later, Tracey charged out of the tent, a hammer in hand. Ruby watched as she skipped across the fallen logs, reaching out as she got close to her husband, resting a hand on his arm. They locked eyes for a second, then she swung, steel meeting bone as she jumped into the fray at last. Ruby allowed herself a small smile.

When the last was felled, and the tired campers had hauled their weary bodies around the campfire, Ruby poured a beer for Tracey first. Raising her chipped mug, she called for silence.

'To new warriors and old, to those who have passed, and those who will join them.' She winked at the woman and drank deeply.

The noise crept up to normal levels once more, sleep mostly for the moment, though Andrew had sent Mick to the community tent to watch some of the younger children as they were sent to get some sleep in the late hour, regardless of his complaints.

Ruby beckoned Eerin over. 'You need to jump on the radio, let the other sites know what happened.'

Eerin nodded and gracefully stood to her full height.

Tracey followed. 'Would you mind showing me how the radio works? If I'm to be of help, I should see where I'll fit.' She directed the question to both of them.

Ruby acquiesced but nodded to her daughter, letting her decide.

'It's fine with me. We could always use the extra help.'

Ruby drank deeply, watching with a smile as the two women vanished behind the tent door.

Tracey peeked out the flap, watching the campfire happily. Eerin twisted the wires, some of them having come loose when the wall shook the nearby cliffs. With every eye focused on the fire, relief lowering their guard, Tracey was the only one to notice the black shadows creeping through the rear of the camp.

'Oh my God, we're saved! The army's here!' she squealed.

Eerin looked up sharply, dropping the wires and darting over to the door. She had barely glanced out when the first shadow reached the group around the fire, just in time to see a glint and a sea of red as Ruby's throat was opened from behind. A woman sitting at the other side of the fire screamed, silenced quickly by another blade as the shadows converged on the group, slaughtering them all before Tracey's excited smile vanished.

Both women started at the carnage, stunned into immobility until they heard the first voice.

'Burn the tents. Burn the bodies. Make sure no one's left.'

The shadows melted into the camp.

Tracey's breath came quick and shallow. Andrew's body swam before her eyes as the air seemed to be sucked out of her. She could hear nothing but the crackle of fire and the beating of her heart. She came back to herself when for the second time that afternoon a hand met her cheek sharply. Her watery eyes met Eerin's, just as teary as her own.

'We have to go. Now.'

'But … Andrew … Mick.'

'Andrew's dead. Mick too probably, along with my mother and daughter. We're alive, and with the radio down, we're the only chance the rest of the group have of survival.' She coughed, the closed air filling up with smoke as the camp burnt around them.

Eerin slipped a knife from her pocket, slicing a jagged tear into the flimsy tent wall and peeking out. She whipped her head back inside as a shadow crept past, then grasping Tracey's sleeve, pulled the woman from the tent and down between the logs they had raced over just an hour before.

Tracey could feel her face, wet with tears. A glance at her companion told her she was no better off.

A whoosh indicated the last of the tents collapsing, as the flames swallowed it up and they turned to the tree line, crawling through the muck, blood and gore as they left their home behind them.

THE SOUTH UNCONQUERED

IN 2017

www.facebook.com/TheSouthForsaken

Acknowledgements

I am overwhelmed with the support I have had from people around me, both overseas and closer to home. Thank you all. Special thanks once again go to Christy, on whom I test every mad idea that runs through my head, and 'our' little zombie podcast family. Your messages of encouragement and enthusiasm keep me going!

For those interested in the zombie genre, I highly recommend you check out these guys:
Zombease.com
Evolution of the apocalypse
(the re-animated) Zpoc nation
Zombieteers
Deadmen talking
The Creepercast
Zombiecast.net

About the Author

Rachel Drummond is the Geelong based author of *The South Forsaken*, and has just released the follow-up, *The South Reclaimed,* to excited fans both close to her home city (the setting for her novels) and internationally.

A lover of reading and horror, she combines her passions with knowledge taken from her work as a nurse to create an apocalypse that will have you looking over your shoulder.

Follow Rachel on Wordpress:
http://racheldrummond2014.wordpress.com